Persona Non Grat

Best Wishes.

Billy Graham

Persona non Grata

Chapter 1

I glanced again at my watch. We had been airborne for over an hour, still not quite half way there.

I looked up at the little girl staring at me over the back of her seat. I smiled and said hello. Her expression never altered, the eyes staring at me taking in every detail of my not so handsome face. I stuck a finger in my ear twisted it and slowly stuck out my tongue. No reaction, hardly a blink. I made what was intended to be a funny face, fully expecting either a loud wee girl laugh or an explosive howl of fright followed by tears and a sharp reprimand from an irate parent at scaring her little angel. Still nothing, she remained impassive, the expression similar to that of a bank clerk when asked for a bank statement, or worse still, a loan.

I closed my eyes hoping she might slide back into her seat. When I opened them again she was still there. I let my eyes wander around but was drawn back to that same little face.

What was she expecting, that my head explode? Or that an ear might suddenly fall off?

Had I a piece of chocolate to offer I could quietly whisper in her ear to bugger off. She was beginning to irritate me.

I never expected that a bad piece of news would come to my aide.

"Afternoon ladies and gentlemen, this is your captain speaking. I am afraid that I have to inform you that due to a lightning strike by Polish Air Control we have been diverted to the nearest airport which in our case is just beyond the Polish border." A slight pause. "I will keep you informed of further developments. In the meantime the cabin crew will provide you with drinks free of charge, and I hope you will enjoy the reminder of your flight."

Amid the rumble of dissension, the old lady sitting across the aisle shook her head disconsolately.

"Now all we need is for the engines to pack in, and we'll be up here all night."

My laughter was out before I could stop it. She looked at me her eyes twinkling, and joined in.

Suddenly she became serious. "I don't have a parachute. Will my brolly do, do you think?"

I pretended to consider. "Could do, you're not too heavy Mary Poppins." We laughed together.

I sat back in my seat. Wee nosey parker had slid back to where she had come, and hopefully would remain there.

I must have dozed, brought back by an unexpected 'dunt' on my shoulder by a stewardess rushing past. I tried to see what was going on further down the aisle but could only make out the same stewardess bending over a seated figure.

"Heart attack," I heard someone whisper.

I closed my eyes and sat back. The intercom came alive. "This is your captain speaking. Have we a doctor on board?"

Whoever had said heart attack was probably correct. Poor sod whoever he or she was, I thought had more to worry about than a controllers strike. Where would we land now?

A few minutes later one of the cabin crew passed.

"Excuse me please," My little parachutist asked as he passed. "Did they find a doctor for our person with the heart attack?"

The young man leaned over her. "Yes madam, but it was not a heart attack. The man has suddenly taken ill. The doctor says he will be all right. There will be an ambulance waiting for him when we land. Okay?"

When he had gone the old lady looked across at me, "An ambulance waiting for him? Maybe they should make that two, I'm rapidly ageing up here."

I dozed again, a useful way to pass the time. This time it was one of the cabin crew who provided us with the information that our estimated time of arrival at the small airport a few miles from the Polish border was around forty minutes from now. We would be staying overnight in accommodation provided by the airline, and as it was not known how long the strike would last we would be required to decide whether to return to Glasgow, or wait and resume our journey to Krakow.

I let out a subdued sigh. I had only packed a small holdall for my five days tour of Krakow intending to visit the concentration camp and the salt mine. Now it was a matter of how long the strike should last, or alternatively, sit in a hotel and wait to be flown back home.

My only consolation was that as a Private Detective, albeit a third rate one, I did not have any employer… or client for that matter to answer to. Therefore once on the ground I'd phone or text my big brother DI Fenton Barns and let him know the score. I smiled already anticipating his answer of '*so you've got yourself into another fine mess, West. Do you want big brother to come and hold your hand as usual?*'

It was closer to an hour rather than the estimated time when we touched down, which looking out appeared to be nothing short of a field, and I wondered if the flight path was lit by tubs of paraffin or whatever else they might have used as they had done in WW2.

As I only had my overnight bag with my few but precious belongings, I did not have to wait at the carousel which I believed to be operated by a wee man somewhere turning a handle.

Waiting at the customs counter I showed my passport, and opened my bag as requested.

"Would you come this way sir," the sour faced official asked me.

The nightmare had begun.

"This is your bag?" the tall slim officer asked, pointing at my sole possession on his small unvarnished desk.

I nodded. "Yes."

"Did you pack it yourself?"

Again I nodded.

"Was it ever out of your sight?"

"Only when I fell asleep on the flight."

The slim officer glared at me not knowing whether I was making a joke or not. Instead his answer to my ill timed humour was to hold up two small white packets for my inspection. "Are these yours?"

This time I shook my head. "No. Never seen them before."

"Then why were they found in your luggage?" His smirk was similar to a poker player who held all the aces.

"Perhaps, someone knowing they would be caught put them there. What are they anyway? Salt? Soap powder?"

"Come come Mr Barns you are not that stupid," he mocked me.

Now tired, angry and impatient, I answered, "Exactly, only a stupid person would leave something like that lying around to be found by someone certainly not stupid such as yourself."

My English had him confused for a minute. To retain his authority, he said. "We will have to detain you Mr Barns for further questioning. Please be good enough to follow my officer." He *pointed* to a young uniformed man who *pointed* his weapon menacingly at me.

"What am I being charged with?" I asked, as if I didn't know.

"Attempting to smuggle drugs for your own use. It is prohibited in my country." The captain answered sternly. To my surprise he handed me my bag. "You may have these for the present."

Reluctantly I thanked him and followed my captor outside to an ominous looking black truck complete with barred windows, and politely invited to step inside.

My journey was short. I sat there clutching my overnight bag my mind swirling at the thought of my forthcoming fate. I, a drug addict! or worse a dealer?

The police station as was had its location in a sleazy part of the town, or what I had seen of the town through the barred window of my transport. With a sinking heart I stepped down from my prison on wheels.

The station's interior matched its external surroundings, stinking with the smell of sweat and stale urine. This time I was unceremoniously pushed into a small office occupied by a small overweight officer who, at my far from dignified entrance sat back in his chair, a half smoked cheroot drooping from the side of his mouth.

"Your passport, if you please." He looked up at me, bored as if having already done this a hundred times.

I reached into my jacket pocket extracted the said document and handed it to him, which he took, flicked through the pages before throwing it down on his desk.

Next he unzipped my bag, extracting first my few clothes on top, which he set to one side on his desk, then my electric razor to the other side, followed by my toiletries. The paperback novel I had started to read on the plane was dropped with a grunt back into my bag.

Clearly disappointed 'obese person' shot a hostile stare up at me, with the command, "empty your pockets."

Reluctantly I rummaged in my jacket pockets and threw a clean white handkerchief on to his desk followed by my key ring, thankful that my front door was a long way away. The officer snapped his knuckles urging me to be quick and I knew what he was after but had no way of refusing. At the sight of my wallet he gave a grunt almost tearing it from my grasp raking through the Euro bank notes until coming to my credit cards, and somehow I had the feeling I would not see them again. Luckily the bank had forewarned me of the procedure, wanting to know of my holiday destination, and happily this was not one of them.

Another snap of his knuckles and I unstrapped my watch. Again I had had the foresight to wear a cheapish make, something in which my esteemed officer was far from happy.

Next he picked up my mobile, studied it briefly and threw it beside my razor.

"You may have back your belongings," he said quietly, then a little louder when I reached for my wallet, razor and mobile, "not those."

"What happens now?" I asked, hiding my apprehension.

The officer sat back in his chair blowing smoke into the already humid air. "You will be charged of course with the possession of drugs." He made no attempt to offer me a seat.

"Am I allowed a phone call, preferably to my embassy?"

The office smiled. "In this I would be most happy to oblige, except there is no British or American embassy in my country."

My heart sank. "Well at least let me inform my travel agent or the airline what has happened to me. They will be worried by my absence."

The officer waved a hand. "Already done, Mr Barns, it is now up to them what course of action they might wish to take."

For a time there was silence in that humid room, the only sound the irregular whirring of the broken fan clinging it would seem for dear life to the ceiling above, while my interrogator wrote hurriedly on a sheet of paper.

Finally finished, he put down his pen and stared at me as if having forgotten that I was there.

"Sergeant take the prisoner down to the cells."

The policeman stepped forward and pointed to the door.

"You will be taken up to the prison Mr Barns and remain there until your appearance in court." The man behind the desk informed me.

I choked back my horror. "When is that likely to be, I'm due back at work on Friday," I said intending to sound flippantly cheerful.

The officer shook his head. "I am afraid not, if convicted you will miss many Fridays, probably for several years to come." He turned to his subordinate. "Constable, take him away."

It was a long narrow corridor that I was taken to, with a wooden bench running its entire length. I sat there facing a row of cells all occupied by what looked like animals in a zoo, all shouting and swearing at me. Without exception all were tattooed as the saying goes 'from arse to elbow' either naked to the waist or wearing a logo bearing vest. All clambering at the bars to eat me alive or do their worst, I suspected the latter.

I felt afraid. To be banged up for a few days…hours even with any of this lot would be disastrous.

I was no kickboxing champion or martial arts expert that could disable half the prison population and therefore become immune to threats, as per Hollywood films. On the contrary I was a slim built thirty something with a gammy leg…reason enough for having retired from my local police force a few years ago. Even big brother Fenton would have his work cut out taming this lot.

An hour passed and the noise and foreign abuse hurled at me had not subsided. Why the hell did not someone come and feed them, give me peace and quiet for a time?

Just then my prayers were answered in the form of my former constable appearing.

He motioned that I should follow him, and I picked up my bag. At the door to the street, a fellow officer was in the act of handcuffing a man, a car had screeched to a halt. A man leapt out, and bundled me into it before my startled captor was aware of what was happening, the second accomplice dealt with the remaining police officer, and my car took off like a bat out of hell with me lying sprawled on the floor in the back, miraculously my bag was somewhere beneath me.

"In the name o' the wee man!"I exploded struggling to rise. "What's going on?"

In answer the car swung round a bend in the street and my head hit the side window with a thump. Next to me a man pulled me unceremoniously into a seat beside him.

"You are all right *gospodine?*"

I sat back and rubbed my head. "I think so..not sure."

This was way and above too much in so short a time from arriving at a rundown airport, and I was not too sure whether I was dreaming and would wake up to a certain little girl staring up at me. And right now I would give the world if that were true.

In the passenger seat, a young dark haired young woman twisted round to face me. "You *are* all right?" She sounded anxious.

"Yes, thanks, but I should like to know what's going on." I took a not too interested look out of the car window. "Is this how you welcome all your visitors to your country?"

Her flicker of a smile lit up a lovely face. "It is, when it is how fat Sergeant Sowa makes a living." The car cut a corner before she could continue. "Sowa would have you sweat up in Zatvor and before your trial was due, would offer to drop all charges for a most reasonable amount." She turned back.

"So that's his little game," I addressed the back of her head. "Do you make it a point to rescue all the poor devils caught in his clutches?"

"No. But you are most important to us."

"Why me? I...."

"You must wait. It will not be too long until we are there."

There followed a dialogue of chatter in my rescuers own language, then silence.

Suddenly tired I sat back in my seat and took a lazy interest at the countryside we were now flashing through at the speed of knots, and I suspected that we were being pursued by my former 'friends'.

I was not wrong, somewhere in the distance a car with a flashing blue light was following.

My lady friend said something to the driver and he suddenly veered off the main road on to a dirt track, which we bounced over for the next twenty or so minutes until he was sure that there was no one behind.

We slowed and I let out a sigh of relief.

I looked around and found that we were surrounded by hills, having left my prison town some distance behind. The driver said something and dropped the car down a steep slope to where two tracks split into different directions. The woman in the front seat pointed to the driver to turn left and we set off down that narrow bumpy road. All the while my thoughts were, that I was travelling further away from the airport and possibly my freedom.

The dirt track that had been chosen eventually led us to a rundown old stone farmhouse, thin blue smoke rising lazily into the air from a crooked chimney.

Our car pulled up at the door and the young woman got out and motioned me to do the same.

In company with the other two occupants of the car I stepped into the semi dark interior of the house.

"Please be seated." The woman said, and I sat down at a far from stable looking wooden chair next to a table.

A burly unsmiling man pushed a cup of coffee across the wooden table to me. I grunted my thanks and took a sip, finding more than coffee in the cup. I coughed and the big man's face broke into a smile.

At the far end of the room, from what I guessed to be the kitchen, a door opened and a man dressed in a white satin shirt entered, and crossed to shake my hand.

"Mr Malcolm. I am pleased that you have agreed to help us. We are sorry about the trouble at the police station. Zofia told me that our Captain Sowa is still up to his old tricks. It could have proved most inconvenient…for us, had we failed to affect your release, and of course yours." He laughed loudly and held out his hand. "My name is Silvo I am leader of this group."

At my look of puzzlement he asked, "you understand my English?"

I nodded. "No trouble there, pal, except my name's not Malcolm, I think you have the wrong guy whoever he is."

As the saying goes you could have cut the air with a knife. My host stared at me in disbelief uttering a few un-English words as he glared at those around him.

Zofia crossed to where I sat at the table. "You are not Mr Malcolm who has come to help our cause?" At my look of astonishment she carried on. "He has much to teach us, also take back to England what we have worked so hard for."

I ran a finger slowly round the rim of my cup. "I'm still not your Mr Malcolm. You've got the wrong delivery."

This I could not understand. My flight was intended to land in Poland so why had they expected to meet this Mr Malcolm here?

She saw that I was puzzled and began to explain. "We heard of the controllers strike and that Mr Malcolm's flight would be diverted here. Originally it was to touchdown at Krakow and our agents were to bring him here." She gave a brief smile. "The strike saved them the trouble. However, it was you who we mistook for our Mr Malcolm as you were the only one to disembark that fitted his description."

It slowly dawned on me how this had come about. "There was a man on the plane who was suddenly taken ill, he must be the Mr Malcolm you expected."

The leader snapped his fingers. "Then all has been explained. The mistake is ours mister....?"

"Barns...West Barns to be precise." I heaved a sigh. "So where do we go from here?"

Silvo shrugged. "That is the problem. Unless of course you know something about weaponry etc."

I made a face "I don't even know anything about etc."

My joke having failed he moved to the centre of the room. "What would you have us do, Mr Barns as you are of no use to us so to speak?"

I didn't much care for the expression describing me as nothing other than *persona non grata*.

"You could return me to the airport. I'm sure the holiday reps will be relieved at my reappearance."

Silvo shook his head. "Our friend Sowa will have that watched. He will not wish to lose his ransom money."

"Ransom money?"

"Yes when you were charged with drug possession Sowa would have you sent to Zatvor prison, in fact that is where you were headed when we rescued you. You see," Silvo folded his arms. "The intention was …as it has always been with those as unfortunate as yourself, that you should be held there until relatives and friends raise the required sum to affect your release. Unfortunately, Sowa and his crew believed you to be of some importance and thus able to raise what they asked, which in some cases amount to fifty thousand American dollars."

I let out a whistle of astonishment faintly smiling at the thought of brother Fenton scurrying about to raise such a large sum. Knowing his sense of humour he was likely to have me sweat it out for a while if even to teach me a lesson. Again when I thought of those animals I had seen behind bars in the police station I could not stop myself from shaking.

"So you don't think I can reach the airport and my rep?" My voice edged with concern.

"No. But even so, do you have your passport?"

I swallowed and choked, "No".

"Just as I suspected."

Before I could ask anything more, the door burst open and a man ages with myself emerged amid the cries of Serge! Serge! from those around and I took him to be some sort of hero.

"Serge!" Zofia cried running to engulf him in her arms, amidst a few calling out what I took to be ribald remarks.

Zofia turned to face me, introducing the newcomer with a broad smile of pride. "This is my…how do you say fiancée."

I smiled back. "Congratulations."

"My name is Serge," the fiancée informed me seriously.

"I gathered that," I smiled. "Pleased to meet you Serge."

"This is Mr Barns, we have mistaken him for Mr Malcolm," Zofia explained.

Serge nodded that he understood then turned to Silvo, probably asking what the hell were they going to do with me, and I hoped the answer was a happy one.

The group leader barked out a few names and they gathered around a table on the farther side of the room, where heads together they presumably were deciding my fate.

Zofia and Serge sat down beside me and the old lady shuffled across to fill up their empty cups, Serge addressing her affectionately.

At length the 'summit ' over, the gathering dispersed, Silvo crossed to deliver the verdict…and presumably my fate.

"We have decided the best course of action is that Serge and Zofia take you to see someone who will know best how to have you return home."

I heaved a sigh of relief.

"We of course must be very careful, you understand?"

"Of course." It seemed that I was about to be dumped on some unsuspecting person, my feeling of not being wanted here equated to my singing at a New Year party, and I vowed that should I ever make it home I would never sing again.

I was not quite sure what it was they 'had to do,' and did not really want to find out. So far all I was sure of was this group were against the government, something that their Mr Malcolm was to help them with, and also to return home with information on what was going on in this little country of theirs, something else I did not want to know.

That was as far as I got with my thoughts. Reason; the loud sound of a motor bike outside and a youngster flying in with the news that soldiers were not very far behind.

Instantly everyone knew what to do, from the old woman swooping up cups and dirty dishes to others quickly disappearing into the hillside, Sofia shouting at me to follow her.

In no time I was back in our car, the same driver gunning us down a rutted road, Zofia in the front seat flashing glances behind her, beside me my fellow passenger checking his automatic weapon.

All this I thought free of charge!

It was ages before we reached a metalled road, where a second government car appeared out of nowhere. Our driver raised our speed and I held on for dear life the hairs on the back of my neck standing (probably surrendering) awaiting that first hail of bullets through the rear window.

It took a few miles before we outdistanced our pursuers and I had just breathed a sigh of relief when rounding a bend, Serge let out a cry of alarm, pointing ahead at what I guessed to be a roadblock. Instantly our driver braked to a halt and switched off the lights in the gathering darkness of a long day.

Slowly he crept forward. Zofia turned to face me. "We must try and drive through. Should things not go well for us make for the bushes. It is up to you from there. My advice is do not get caught. Not now. Good luck."

Suddenly the car jerked forward heading at full speed at what appeared to be a makeshift barrier of barrels and bits and pieces, which is how I thought we would end if we didn't make it. The driver swore, gunned the car even faster, and we were through, dull thuds filling the inside of our car, outside, barrels flying in different directions or rolling past.

Serge let out a yell of triumph I expelled relief, thinking what next, having momentarily forgotten our recent pursuer.

We accelerated, in contrast to the car following, having to slow down to wind its way through the debris strewn road, giving us time to put a greater distance between us, which we did until approaching the outskirts of at first glance what appeared to be a fairly large town.

Our driver slowed, turning into a narrow street, but now our adversaries were not so far behind. He accelerated, spinning the wheel and we shot up another narrow but this time a steep street. I hoped he knew what he was doing as I believed that at any time we would find ourselves in a dead end, with the emphasis on dead. However we made it. The driver swung right, and a few streets more, right again, then again, quickly drawing up at the corner to sit there with the engine idling.

A few minutes passed and we took off again, our driver grunting with satisfaction at our pursuers flashing past at the top of the street. He had driven round in a circle and now the other car was chasing its own tail.

Chapter 2

It was dark when we halted at the iron gates of a large house. Serge got out and opened them to let us through, and we drove to the top of the driveway, where we got out, the car quickly disappearing out of sight round the back.

The large entrance hall led to the foot of a winding staircase where a refined looking middle aged man came to welcome us.

Zofia greeted him no doubt explaining who I was and how I came to be there.

The man nodded that he understood and held out his hand to me. "I am pleased to make your acquaintance Mr Barns."

"Thank you" I said shaking his hand.

"Come we have much to talk about."

Though he had spoken in English it was to the company that he referred, motioning them to precede him into the large lounge.

A manservant appeared from nowhere with steaming hot coffee on a tray.

Serge lifted a cup. "We must get Mr Barns back home."

Our host nodded. He turned to me. "We cannot do this immediately. We have much more business to attend to, you will understand, you having arrived unexpectedly in our midst so to speak."

"Sorry about that," I apologised. "Blame the Poles," I half smiled.

"Quite. So we must think of a way to get you to the border. You have no passport, I take it?"

"No. I was relieved of that at the police station, Mr ?"

"You may call me Mark," he smiled.

Mark took a step away from the unlit fire where he'd stood. "I will have Alex bring you something to eat while we discuss our business in the other room."

Thank the wee man for that I thought, I'm starving. I looked up at Mark from where I sat. "Take your time, I'm not going anywhere," I grinned.

It was an hour later before the door opened and they filed into the room.

"You have eaten I see." Mark indicated my empty plate.

"Yes thank you, I really appreciated it."

He sat down on a leather chair by the fireside, the others finding seats in the large room.

"I have…we," he corrected himself, "have decided the best plan is for you to remain here, until our very important business has been completed." He hesitated, choosing his words carefully, "then we will endeavour to help you to the Polish border."

I swallowed afraid to ask how long. Mark anticipated my question. "That should only be a day or two. Until then consider this as your home."

With that they gathered round Mark to say their goodbyes, Zofia saying that she hoped to see me soon.

Their leaving left the place with a feeling of emptiness.

Mark returned from having seen them on their way. "You should wish a nightcap I think the impression is?"

I nodded. "That would just about see an end to my very busy but not uneventful day." I stifled a yawn while my host crossed to the drinks cabinet.

"You would like vodka?" he turned and held up a bottle.

"You wouldn't come to have my home grown brew by any chance?" I asked hopefully.

Mark turned back to the cabinet. "That would be?"

"Whisky. Scotch to you." I said to his back. I heard him chuckle and turn round holding a half full glass of the amber nectar.

He crossed and handed me the glass. "Cheers," I said raising my glass.

He looked at me as if having never before heard the expression. You're lucky I thought, that I didn't say *here's tae us, wha's like us.*

He sat down across from me. "I suppose that to be suddenly thrust into... let's say you don't know what, you are asking yourself what all this is about." He halted while I sipped my drink, and waited for him to continue.

"It is better that you do not know." He halted expecting me to say something. At my silence he went on, "It is something not many in your country would know anything about... or wish to know." The man took a sip of his drink. "You are here on holiday?"

"No. Poland, Krakow."

"Ah! the salt mine and no doubt the concentration camp." He stared at me knowingly. "Should our work here against the government fail, then this my friend will also become a camp such as that."

Mark saw me wrinkle my brows. "That is why your Mr Malcolm was invited, to let the world know what is happening here."

"And the weaponry?"

"We cannot fight oppression solely with our bare fists."

I sighed. "It must have been a bit of a shock when you got me instead."

Mark laughed. "As you say, a bit."

He stood up. "But you are tired, I will have Alex show you to your room. Unfortunately I must leave you tomorrow for my office." Then sternly, "on no account must you be seen. Please do not leave the house, even to venture into the back garden."

I was in the hallway when I saw the phone. Instinctively and without thinking I uttered, "a phone!" and stretched out my hand, only to have it jerked aside and my host barking at me, "What the hell do you think you are doing?"

Taken by surprise by the severity of the voice I took a step back. Perhaps all of this was not what I was led to believe.

What if these people were no more than a gang of criminals, and I was now a prisoner in this house?

"I simply want to phone my rep and tell her that I'm alright, and that I've lost my passport and can she help to get me out of this damned country," I finished angrily.

"Then what? The papers get hold of it, your picture plastered all over the front page! Police chasing you and *us*!"

I simmered down having seen his point. "I'm sorry I wasn't thinking."

"That could get you shot here, Mr Barns."

"What about my brother?" I asked hopefully, "I could explain how precarious my position is here. He would understand, most probably be able to do something about it." *Like hiring a helicopter* I thought to myself.

My host too had calmed down. "I am sorry Mr Barns...West, I cannot take the chance. All calls out of the country are monitored, or so I am led to believe. Unfortunately, there are more lives than mine to consider. I just cannot take the risk."

Mark took a step away, once again in control of his temper. "Get a good night's sleep and we'll talk again in the morning. Breakfast is at eight. Good night. Alex will show you to your room."

My room as was the rest of the house, large, and this evening hot, it not yet having cooled from a warm August day.

I sat down on the edge of the big double bed, wishing that when I woke up in the morning it would be in my own room in North Berwick, and I followed these thoughts with a mouthful of curses at ever having thought of this holiday.

Holiday! Anything but.

I yawned and raked through my holdall. At least I had a clean shirt and a few toiletries, so I wouldn't stink to high heaven for a day or two. To further calm my brain I contemplated on reading my novel but dropped it back into my bag, unable to recall what chapter I had last read and what the plot was all about, no doubt not as deep and complicated as my own.

Finally I undressed and lay down, gradually drifting into sleep on how I was ever to get to the Polish border, or more importantly stay alive.

Next morning I rose and made my way to the dining room where my host already sat at breakfast. At my entrance he looked up from his newspaper and greeted me warmly, our little altercation from the previous night obviously forgotten.

"You slept well, West?"

"Yes thank you." I sat down across from him, and Alex placed a plate of cheese and some sort of biscuit and small cakes in front of me."

Mark saw me stare at them. "Not your usual I take it?" he smiled.

I shrugged. "No"

Mark rose. "You must excuse me, I have to leave for work now. I must live as normal a life as possible you will understand. Fortunately my owning the Company gives me leeway to come and go as I please. This way, Zofia who works for me is not under suspicion when I send her on errands that necessitate her absence for a day or two." His voice hardened. "I must again warn you of the danger your being here puts me…my group in. Please do as I have said, keep away from the windows or the urge to go outside," he hesitated, "or the phone."

"I know what you are saying. But how long will I be here? And do you have any idea how to get me out?"

"I am working on it, West." He drew himself up, "Believe me I am as anxious to see you leave as you are to be home again."

My host was at the door before he spoke again. "More so now, that the farmhouse where first you were taken and had to so suddenly leave was raided, and the old lady shot for helping us. So you see this is not a game that we are playing Mr West Barns, or if it is, it is one of life and death." He closed the door behind him.

It was a long boring day and I was glad when Mark came home, however I ate alone, he having others things on his mind.

I selected a chair in the lounge and at first absently watched TV, which I had done at intervals during the day, only to be continually frustrated by the dubbing of English speaking films preventing me from following the dialogue. Suddenly my interest was drawn to pictures of police and soldiers on a country road milling around what appeared to be two lifeless. bodies, lying there.

Just then Mark came into the room, saw what I was looking at, saying as he sat down in what I took to be his favourite chair. "It all went wrong. It all went wrong."

I sat silent, thinking better not to ask.

Just then the doorbell rang, and I heard Alex's voice, then that of Serge. A few seconds later Serge came in followed by Zofia, both looked pale and drawn.

Mark did not rise to greet them but instead gestured despairingly. "Help yourselves to a drink, also a Scotch for West," he said in English.

Serge did as he was asked, crossing to the drinks cabinet while Zofia seated herself in a chair a little way from her boss.

"What went wrong?" their leader asked, looking up at Serge and taking the drink from him.

Zofia answered while Serge crossed to hand her a glass of wine. "We were on the wrong road. They were waiting for us."

"The wrong road? How did that come about? The information we received said that was the right road. So how could it have been wrong?"

Serge returned to the cabinet. "Somehow they must have got word of our intentions and switched roads, but lay in wait for our coming."

I was following their conversation none having out of politeness reverted to their own language.

Serge's hand shook as he handed me my whisky.

"We lost two men, boss," Zofia said quietly. Mark raised his brows, waiting for her to go on. "Gorg is phoning from a public box warning their wives to get out of there." She saw Mark stare at her. "No they did not have anything on them that would lead them to us, but they will eventually. They always do."

Mark nodded. "You did right, Zofia."

The door opened and a man of about Zofia's age came in, acknowledging Mark with a slight bow.

"What news do you bring Andrias?"

At first the man appeared surprise to be asked the question in English, until aware of me sitting there quietly sipping my drink, tore his eyes away from Zofia, who he had sought out since his arrival. "We were almost at the junction where we were to intercept the prison vehicle when the first line of fire hit us." He halted while Serge handed him a drink, and I was impressed by the young man's command of English. "Our driver was hit and the car spun off the road. I was thrown free and managed to crawl through the undergrowth and make my escape in the darkness."

For once Marks look darkened. "You made your escape? Did you not wait to see what happened to the others?" he asked angrily.

"Guy was already dead. The driver...I do not know his name..."

"Nor were you supposed to," Mark bit at him.

"He was hit as I said, but I think he was killed when the car spun out of control." The young man pleaded, clasping and unclasping his hands in despair.

"*You think* ! You *only* think!" Mark exploded. "Should he still be alive and talk we are all done for. Why did you not wait and make sure? You know the rules, no one is to be taken alive!"

Aware that he had shocked me by his outburst, Mark reverted to his own language, while I sat there digesting what the implications could mean for me. God help me, this was getting worse by the second.

Eventually a modicum of optimism I suspected returning, Mark's group rose and wishing me a polite good night left, Serge with the glimmer of a smile.

A little later, sitting at supper, Mark spoke in a tone intended to assure me, "I know what we must do is harsh.. even savage, but it is nothing to what the Federal soldiers will do should any of us fall into their hands. Tonight's operation was to free our men on their way to execution. Those same men suffered hours, days of torture, yet none gave us away. It might not always be the case. Do you understand?"

I picked at my food. "Yes I believe I do, and I don't envy you the decisions you might have to make."

"Good. As co coordinator of five groups I must think what is best overall. My greatest frustration is that I cannot personally take part in any of the operations."

My host rose. "It vexes me to see the situation you are in through no fault of your own. When this has simmered down I will once again make arrangements to have you reach the border, but once again I ask you to be patient and diligent."

That night I lay in bed wondering whether I would ever reach Poland. Despite Mark's reassurance that no harm would come to me, I had no qualms that should the situation arise whereby my presence was a danger to his groups he would have no hesitation in having me dealt with.

I clasped my hands behind my head and stared up at the white ceiling as if hoping to see the solution there. I could of course attempt to make my own way to the border, except I had no money, and my appearance was strictly foreign. Should my circumstances become more desperate I would use the house phone. At least that way I was sure, well almost sure to reach Fenton, then take it from there.

However next morning altered everything completely. I was sitting at breakfast when Mark entered the room.

"Good morning West, I think you will wish to see this." He threw the newspaper down on the table in front of me.

"Morning Mark." I looked up at him at the same time lifting the paper. There on the front page was a photo of myself.

Mark sat down. "It says that your embassy in Poland is investigating your disappearance. They state that according to your holiday company, you were last seen escorted away by two uniformed policemen. Since then your whereabouts are unknown."

I felt a sudden surge of hope at this. "So what now? Surely they will find out that our fat friend had me held for drug possession."

"Sowa will deny it of course. He must protect himself, and most importantly not a few of his superiors who are also involved in his little sordid scheme. And we cannot verify your arrest without implicating ourselves."

"I could buy a mobile or phone the embassy from a public call box," I said hopefully.

"You could. But how would explain where you have been all this time?"

Mark looked steadily at me having no need to elaborate, and I had the feeling that no British Ambassador would have any jurisdiction here. My only hope was to contact Fenton and explain the position to him, who in turn could do the same by contacting the correct channels at home. However I had an uneasy feeling this man here would find a way to prevent me from doing just that.

"Leave things as they are, West, I have already put your leaving us into motion. This," he pointed to the newspaper "greatly helps our cause.

Chapter 3

My five days holiday had expired. That is the five days that I should have spent in Krakow seeing the sights and living it up. Now more than ever my brother Fenton would be worrying about my welfare…not to mention my whereabouts.

It happened suddenly, taking me completely by surprise. Mark burst into the lounge, well perhaps burst was an overstatement but certainly more buoyant that normal.

"Go to your room West, you are leaving."

"You mean right now?" I asked, unable to believe this was finally happening.

"Yes, leave your own jacket and wear the one left there for you. Also, I am afraid you must leave your holdall behind. Use the backpack we have provided, you must blend in with those around you. You will also need this." he handed me what I knew to be a passport. "It is Polish, your British one was too difficult to come by." He pointed to the photo. It was the same as one of me in the newspaper. "I said it would come in useful," he grinned.

Then serious again, explained. "First you will be driven to Zepa. My men will obtain a railway ticket for you. They will not accompany you on the train as it does not halt at the border. Fortunately all documents are inspected en route. Should you be stopped, you will sign that you are a deaf mute."

He handed me a roll of banknotes. I took them, thanking him. "I don't know if I can ever return the money to you, that is without getting you into trouble."

"It is of no consequence. The fault is mainly ours. Take what little you have." He smiled. "You never know you might find the time to finish that book you brought with you."

I returned his smile, happy that I was leaving. "Maybe. I'm still not halfway through it."

I was back in five minutes with not as much as a sigh at leaving my room, though hoping to have left all my fears and trepidations there.

Mark walked with me round the side of the house where two men stood beside a not so new car. "This is Josef." He introduced me to a small thin shabbily dressed man, who merely nodded but made no attempt to shake my outstretched hand. *Not much of a good start, I thought feeling embarrassed.* "He is your driver. Andrias you have already met from the other night." Mark referred to the second man who stepped forward to shake my hand warmly.

To myself I thought, *let's hope this little escapade ends better than your last one, Andrias my good man.*

The little man was first into the car sitting in the driver's seat and Andrias with a final few words to Mark got in beside him.

Mark held out his hand. "Have a safe journey Mr West Barns. You will understand me if I say I hope we do not meet again."

"Or if we do it's in more pleasant circumstances," I amended.

"Quite." With a wave he walked away.

We did not talk much on the journey, Andrias asking if was true that it always rained in Scotland, and me answering, no that it sometimes snowed instead. He laughed. "You drink Scotch to keep warm."

"Not at the price it is," I replied.

For a few minutes he sat silent "Have you ever seen the monster?"

I thought for a moment wondering which one he meant my having met a few, but not any he was likely to know.

He saw me hesitate. "You know? the one in the big lake."

"Oh!" I nodded "you mean the Loch Ness Monster."

He nodded vigorously, "yes, yes."

"Sorry to disappoint you pal, no, not ever."

My answer appeared to disappoint him, having no doubt expected me to tell him how it reared its head out of the water terrifying locals, while looking for an English tourist to devour.

It was the end of our conversation until our silent driver pulled up in a side street a little distance away from the bustling railway station.

My excitement rose at getting closer to my destination which in my case was any part of Poland.

I got out of the car shouldered my backpack and waited for my escorts. Together we walked as casually as the others towards the station, Andrias saying quietly, "I shall go for the tickets. When I return I will point out the platform you must go to. OK? Show your ticket when you pass through the gate, nod and smile, that is all, do not attempt to say anything."

"No worries pal, I am not likely to say how is Captain Sowa these days."

Andrias left for the ticket office. My little driver indicated his need for the toilet and I sat down on a bench looking interestedly around me, happy to be on my way home. Then it came to me. I had money, why not try and phone Fenton?

I sprang up searching my jacket for my holiday brochures and the emergency phone codes.

There in a corner stood a kiosk, but the money I had was all in notes and I suspected that it would require coins. 'The ball was burst' as the old Scots saying goes.

However I hurried to it, threw open the door and let my eyes fly over the coin box and the row of 10, 15, 20 coin slots.

I stepped back out and looked around me, a few steps away there was a newspaper stand. I walked quickly towards it extracting a bank note from my roll. At the stand I lifted up a newspaper and handed it to the assistant, who with a look of indifference handed me my change. Step one had been achieved.

I hurried back to the kiosk, swearing at the sight of someone inside. Took a hasty look around for my two accomplices, knowing their return could be imminent, and quickly extracting my holiday brochure from my pocket stepped into the now empty box.

Lifting the receiver my eyes flew over the coin slots, and I decided to insert the largest denomination coin that I had, hearing it drop as I dialled the first number, then a hand covered mine and Andrias was quietly ordering me to put the phone down.

Angrily, Andrias glared at me, as I stepped out of the booth. "You should not have attempted to do that Mr West Barns; it was most stupid."

I followed him back to the bench where he had first left me, my little driver shaking his head in disappointment at what I had attempted to do.

Andrias thrust the rail ticket at me, took a glance at his watch stood up and said coldly, "follow me."

Above the usual noise of a busy station, a shrill whistle sounded of an engine anxious to be away. Andrias glared at me, fear in his eyes and without speaking took off, my driver swinging around to face two plain clothes men rushing towards us.

In a flash the little driver was blasting away at his nearest target, the second's man shot swinging him round, before a second shot brought him to the ground.

Instinctively I too ran, expecting to feel the pain of a bullet in my back. I reached a corner, women screamed, others scattered as I roughly pushed aside all those who happened to be in my way. Then I was outside, running to quickly lose myself amongst the crowd, before steeling myself to slow down to a walk and mingle amongst shoppers and other pedestrians.

I crossed the busy street, stole a quick glance behind, no one appeared to be following so I walked casually to where I thought our car was parked. It was, but Andrias was not.

Now what to do? Across the street a café stood on the corner. I made for it and once there took off my backpack and sat down at one of the empty pavement tables where I had a good view of the street and our car parked a little distance away, all the while waiting for Andrias to appear.

My eyes were still on the car when the waiter asked for my order. I choked and looked up at him, asking without thinking 'Snapps.'

Without speaking he took my order and disappeared inside. Sweating, my eyes never having left our car, the temptation was to walk to it in the forlorn hope that I'd find the keys inside.

A hand cut through my vision by the waiter setting down my drink on the table, and saying something that I clearly did not understand, smiled politely and walked away.

I had ordered a drink, therefore could not pretend to be a deaf mute. I took a gulp and set the almost empty glass down. Boy I could go the same again, but dare not push my luck. Besides, I had to have my wits about me, however few they may be.

It was as I downed what was left of my drink that out of the corner of my eye I saw Andrias walking towards the car. Hurriedly I stood up, grabbed my back pack and fumbled in my pocket for the money to pay my drink.

My waiter saw me and I pushed a bank note at him and hurried past, afraid that Andrias would drive away without me. Behind me my waiter shouted something while I crossed the street and I kept on going, all the while my eyes riveted on the car.

I got into the car as Andrias slipped into the driver's seat, at my sudden unexpected appearance he gave a start.

"Surprised to see me big man?" I chuckled while he started up the car. "I think we should get out of here fast, I don't know what my waiter was on about but he didn't look too happy. Maybe I underpaid him for my drink."

Andrias looked startled. "You were in a café?"

"Yip. I had to wait somewhere for you." I looked to see where we were headed. "How did you get away?"

Andrias turned into the main thoroughfare. "I was lucky. I got out by the side entrance."

"How did they know we were there?" was my next question.

"God knows,"Andrias replied, shifting gear.

"And who else, Andrias?" angry and disappointed at my escape having failed, besides that of my near capture.

"Only Mark, our driver Josef and myself."

"What about Zoifia, Serge?"

Andrias nodded. "Probably Zofia. Mark might have found it necessary to tell her. Serge…mm," he wiggled his fingers. "Zofia might have told him."

"And Uncle Tom Cobbly and all."

Briefly Andrias took his eyes off the road to stare at me. I explained, "I mean your security is not really up to scratch is it? Almost everyone knew about us being at the station."

"No. it is not possible. Mark is a very how do you say... cautious leader."

I sat back in my seat and closed my eyes. "Well someone surely did. I'm sure our driver's dead." I stared out of the side window. "One more thing Mark has to worry about.

Now get us home, Andrias, I can't wait to see the look on your boss's face when he sees *me* again."

I was right. Standing in the lounge, Mark jerked his head up at Alex's announcement of my unexpected arrival.

He got to his feet, and looking past me, his face like thunder, asked. "You are alone? Where is Andrias? Has anything happened to him?"

Uninvited I sat down. "No, he's Okay. Right now he's on his way home. He said he'd dump the car where it'll not be traced." Alex handed me a drink.

"What happened?" Mark sat down, his eyes glaring at me and all the trouble I had caused.

"We were almost at the gate of the platform when we were approached by two men. Josef must have sensed trouble and drew his gun. They shot him." I said without emotion.

"And Andrias?"

For a moment I was tempted to voice my puzzlement at the way Andrias had hesitated; granted, only briefly, but stopped myself, by deciding that by telling this already angry man it would in no way improve the situation.

"There wasn't anything he could do but take to his heels as I did. I made my way back to the car and waited until he turned up which he did and he drove me back here."

"I see." Then to Alex hovering in the background. "Alex, fetch Mr Barns something to eat."

It was Mr Barns now I noticed not West. "You are hungry I take it?"

I shrugged "a little something would be appreciated."

I laid the money he had given down on the coffee table. "Thanks for the money. You'll find it all there except for the price of a Snapps."

"Thanks," he said surly but made no attempt to pick it up.

Once again I was back in the room I had come to hate, not the décor or any other thing for that matter, only what it stood for, in my case abject failure. Perhaps things would look different in the morning.

They didn't. Mark had left for work before I came down for breakfast, Alex too, had disappeared.

Again I found myself in the library amongst so many books that I could not understand, only a few having any sort of pictures. I smiled at remembering the books I had been given as a child to keep me quiet while the 'big people' chatted away, books such as the telephone directory or the 'wild lives of birds'. The only kindness shown had been to take the book from me to hold it the right way up. Here I was again in the same dilemma.

Although the situation between Mark and myself was short of cordial, I still looked forward to his company when he returned home at night. The last two nights our conversation had been brief, Mark excusing himself by saying that he had a lot of work to catch up on, leaving me to watch unintelligible TV. My only hope, that perhaps there would be an item of news on my unexplained disappearance. There was none. I was forgotten, no longer newsworthy or even worse 'censored' by this country's government.

Chapter 4

It was the third night after my unsuccessful attempt to escape that Mark's attitude towards me changed. He came into the lounge where I sat disinterestedly trying to fathom the workings of a plot in Polish on TV.

"You leave tomorrow West. Take the same things with you."

"Where to this time?"

"You will first go to one of our hideouts in the mountains from where we will attempt to have you taken to the coast."

I took my eyes off the screen. "Good. So you will provide me with a snorkel or something and point me towards Poland. Or am I left to surfboard my way there?"

To my surprise Mark smiled at my sarcasm. "No. We will think of something more appropriate."

"You said we. What exactly do you mean by that?"

"My organisation."

"Who knows of this Mark? It seems too many people know of your plans for me."

Mark's face darkened. Perhaps it was not so very clever of me to anger him, the only man who could help me.

"Andrias will take you."

My heart jumped a little. "Just him no one else?"

"You will be safe enough with Andrias, he knows what he's doing. When all is clear I will have Zofia come, pick you up in the mountains and take you to the coast."

"How long will that be?

"Not long, perhaps a week."

I thought it might do to put a little pressure on my host. "Not any longer I hope. I'm sure my brother will be doing his best to have the authorities find out what has happened to me, for all I know they might suspect that I have been murdered."

If I had thought to frighten the man I was wrong.

"Then they must start with our Captain Sowa."

"And if they do will it not lead them to you?"

Mark remained calm, aware of what I was trying to do. "No. Sowa will maintain you have been abducted by we terrorists which I believe he has already done, but to where, he has no way of knowing. We might have killed you by this time, having decided there was nothing to achieve by keeping you alive." He smiled a little. "It is not that we could hold you to ransom."

I should not have begun that line, I had only succeeded in confusing myself. However one thing I had learned from it was that Sowa had admitted to my being in his custody and terrorists had freed me, so if the British authorities were in fact looking for me it was evidently the place to start.

"Perhaps now is the time to reappear on Sowa's doorstep, he couldn't very well have me sent to prison, not with the entire world watching…well maybe not the entire world…maybe at least a headline in my local paper." I said amused by the thought.

"Do you want to take that chance? After all you were arrested of being in possession of drugs. And I must warn you, in the past, foreign ambassadors have found it most difficult to affect a release."

I was beaten and Mark knew it. My idea of marching up to the fat captain's door in an attempt to announce to the world my return was never going to work, this and the fact I was not willing to take the risk.

To signify that I was beaten I merely said, "When do I leave with Andrias?"

We started early the next day with Andrias at the wheel. We spoke very little at first, both purposely avoiding our previous little escapade.

After about an hour of small talk and Andrias's history lesson of the surrounding area, and once out of the small towns we had passed through, he pulled up.

"I think I will have a short rest." He opened his car door. "There is a flask of coffee and some sandwiches in the back, you will like them, my wife made them."

I thanked him and reached for the small basket, one eye on Andrias walking away from the car probably to relieve himself.

I opened the flask and poured out some coffee, swithering whether to wait for Andrias's return and wait while he helped himself to a cup of his own coffee. Or perhaps his stopping here on this quiet tree lined road was where he intended to put an end to my unwelcome presence, having caused Mark and his group enough trouble. With more than a little apprehension, I waited expecting him to call me to him. (with probably a gun in his hand).

I unwrapped the sandwiches and relaxed while Andrias walked back to the car. I bit into one and sat there nonchalantly, or appeared to do so, though inwardly shaking while he got back behind the wheel.

"These sandwiches *are* good Andrias. My compliments to your good woman."

He looked puzzled by my flowery language. "Tell your wife she makes good sandwiches."I explained.

"Oh, thank you, I shall tell her as you say."

It was a long journey and with every mile my heart sank at the realisation that I was travelling further away from the Polish border. Where was this damned place? And why was I being taken there? I decided to ask my driver.

"This place, Andrias, what is it really?"

Andrias stared ahead concentrating on the road that was gradually winding up, not a hillside, but a mountain, and looking through my side window saw how high we had travelled. It sure as hell was a long way to 'bump me off.'

"It is where we hide those who are being hunted by our government, or who have been injured."

"I suppose I fit somewhere in between. How long will I be here?" I took a look at a landscape that was rapidly growing more mountainous and barren the higher we drove.

"That is up to Mark. All I know is that I must return home as soon as possible. We all have other jobs in order to make a living. Neighbours notice this you know."

I sighed and sat back in my seat. "As you say, I suppose so."

"Oh we will have to stop!"

Ahead the road was blocked with a few small boulders. We got out and together rolled them down the hillside.

"I take it the council don't have road maintenance away up here," I laughed. Andrias stared at me vacantly. "Never mind Andrias it was a poor joke."

Back in the car my driver started cautiously and it was as well that he did for once again we were out shifting a few more boulders and the occasional rock.

"Not many use this road I would say, Andrias." I sat back glad of the rest.

"Not many. At least the way will be clear for my return." He started the car.

"When will that be?"

"Tomorrow, I hope. I must be back at work next day."

"No rest for the wicked, eh?"

"I beg your pardon, Mr Barns, I am not at all wicked. I do my duty and fight for my country," Andrias answered haughtily.

"Sorry," I apologised. "I didn't apply that you were. It's merely a saying we have."

"Okay. I accept you apology." He tossed his head back a little. "Pour out some coffee, we must not stop again. It will be dark soon and I do not want to drive in these mountains when I cannot see the road."

We continued to drive until reaching a narrow pass. Without warning Andrias drew to a halt.

Slowly he got out of the car and stood there. Somehow I thought that I should do the same.

Despite the recent heat of the day, up here it was cold with a wind whistling through the pass. Andrias stood looking anxiously around him, and I was about to ask him why, when out of the gathering mist a figure appeared, a large armed hostile looking man, attired in a knee length sheepskin coat walking cautiously towards us.

"Shep!" Andrias called out cheerfully hurrying to meet him. I waited by the car feeling a little relieved that this fierce looking individual was on our side so to speak.

After they had embraced, Andrias turned to wave me to come and meet his friend.

I smiled warmly or as warmly as I could, and it was not the wind that prevented me from doing so. This man might be Andrias's friend and also that of Mark, but the sight of him armed to the teeth gave me a sinking feeling in the pit of my stomach that I was being led to nothing other than an armed rebel camp. Now I was really mixed up in the ongoing revolution, or whatever it may be called. *Where are you Fenton?, and if you are anywhere near I hope it is in a helicopter.*

Andrias's friend made no attempt to shake my hand, but merely accepted my presence with a grunt before turning back to speak to Andrias.

Greetings over we walked back to the car.

"Your pal's not a very good singer," I said, walking round a small boulder.

"My friend doesn't sing," Andrias answered puzzled.

"Nor does he smile or shake hands." I thought it was about time I made some effort not to be taken as a silent pawn in some game Mark and his friends were playing, even should that indeed be in helping me.

"We must all be suspicious of strangers." Andrias said defensively.

"Me included?" I asked, my hand on the car door.

Andrias shrugged. "Mark's orders were to bring you here, until it is safe to get you over the border."

"How far away is that?"

"Many kilometres. It will be Zofia's job to take you there." He slid into the driver's seat. "Come, we must reach our destination before it grows dark."

Andrias started the car and a few yards further on came upon what I took to be our recent guard's motor bike standing against a rock, which gave me the impression that we were still some distance away from our destination. I was right, a mile further on, glancing up at the hillside above I caught sight of what could only be described as a machine gun nest, obviously the place was well fortified and camouflaged, then we were descending into a tree filled gully, strangely out of contrast to the surrounding countryside.

Andrias followed, what was to me an almost invisible track, coming at length and quite suddenly to three fairly large wooden buildings nestling under tall Fir trees, or maybe Pine, being no expert on either fauna or flora I did not really know, and at this stage care.

We left the car and walked to the door of the nearest building, unlit as were the other two, the buildings made even darker in the approaching darkness under the canopy of trees.

We were almost at the door when it opened, and I was certain our approach had been well watched, only the merest glimmer of light showed from behind the giant of a man who stood there, his attire similar to our mountain guard.

"Andrias," the deep voice of the big man boomed at us.

"Castra," my companion called back cheerfully.

I followed Andrias, and the giant stood back to let me enter.

The room was large, a long rough table occupied the centre, with bunk beds lining two walls. The place reminded me of one of those old WW2 war films of prison camps. Curious faces stared at me as though I had two heads or some other disfigurement, my presence breaking the previous loud chatter of two score or more greedily enjoying their evening meal.

Andrias!" someone shouted cheerfully, with others quickly following.

Smiling broadly at his popularity Andrias introduced me to the entire company who in turn acknowledged my presence with polite gestures, or what I hoped were polite gestures, though I had experienced something similar but with quite different connotations in one or two pubs back in East Lothian.

Those sitting nearest shuffled along on their wooden benches to make room for us. I showed my gratitude, removed my backpack and sat down.

A bowl of soup of some sort was quickly pushed in front of me. But when you're hungry some sort will do, and by the look of this soup this was indeed 'some sort.' I picked up a spoon and someone handed me a large piece of brown bread. I thanked whoever it was and started to eagerly spoon my broth. It *was* good, then again when you're hungry anything tastes good.

"It is good?" Andrias nudged my elbow urging me to acknowledge the big man across the table who had asked the question.

Even if it had not been I was in no position to contradict him. Still supping I nodded eagerly, to ensure that I would not be next on the menu.

I had scarcely finished before a huge mug of coffee was thrust at me. Again I showed my gratitude.

"We must make our presence known to Arnau," Andrias urged me to quickly finish my drink.

"Arnau?" I asked.

"Yes he is the leader. We must meet him and explain why Mark wants you here."

We left, crossing to a smaller building not unlike a ski lodge.

The man we met was a burly man of just under six feet tall. Andrias greeted him explaining who I was, fortunately for me he spoke English but addressed himself to my companion in a way that left me in no doubt that my presence here was unwelcome.

"You expect me to look after him? Feed him? What use is he here, other than to have more authorities searching for us."

"Mark should like to be rid of him as well, that is why Zofia will be here in a day or two to take him to the coast, where it is hoped he will make his way home." Andrias explained almost in a frightened way.

"Until then I must look after him, as if I had nothing better to do, and share what little food we have?"

I had had enough of this man talking as if I was not there. "Excuse me," I started sharply, "Remember me the invisible man?" Both halted to stare at me, and I continued, "I'm not exactly happy to be here myself in your *wonderful country* and the quicker I can get home to mine the happier I will be." My next tirade I aimed at the leader. "So just tell me what you want me to do, and I'll do it."Adding sarcastically. "And, I'll fast if you want me to, I can do without eating too many hamburgers you know."

For a moment Arnau stood there expressionless, then suddenly his laughter filled the small room. He stepped forward and shook my hand vigorously. "My apologies mister Englishman, you must forgive my lack of manners."
"And I will forgive you for calling me an Englishman, for as much as you are not Polish, neither am I English, but Scottish."

"Ah where you?" he mimicked someone playing the bagpipes.

Relieved that I would not have this man to contend with as an enemy, I readily laughed.

Andrias woke me early next morning. "I must go now, West." He looked down at me from where he stood.

I yawned up at him from my bunk bed. "Good luck, Andrias. Thanks for bringing me here."

Though it was not the place I would have chosen, at least, I hoped, it was a step closer to home.

"It might be a day or two before Zofia calls for you, or she would have brought you here herself. I think Mark's plan is for her to take you to the coast and try and have you reach Poland from there. However you must make the best of it here," he said sympathetically.

I swung my legs and sat on the edge of the bed. "Have you filled your flask? It's a long way back. Remember to be careful." I did not know what else to say, to show my appreciation, and dispel a little of my own distrust of the man.

"Yes. I will be. I have a family to think about. Also I must get back to work."

He turned away. "Perhaps we may meet again some day. Perhaps in that country of yours."

"Maybe," I smiled up at him. "You never know." Then he was gone, leaving me alone in a place where I would rather not be. A place I believed was not taking me closer to home but rather, deeper into the world of intrigue and betrayal.

That same afternoon I took a stroll around the small camp, until my legs took me involuntary into the surrounding woods. Here it was pleasant in the cathedral silence amongst the tall trees. I heard the snap of a twig and swung round to face the rugged shape of a man pointing a sub machine gun in my direction. I gave him what I hoped was a friendly wave. In answer his wave was with his gun, and not at all friendly. He took a couple of steps towards me, and by his angry tone I guessed this was not a place I was supposed to be.

I gestured that I understood, hoping to sound cheerfully understanding as I turned away. "Okay pal, no need to lose the heid (head) I'm on my way. I wasna wanting to steal any of your trees anyway. You can count them if you want."

Stupid bugger I thought, what am I going to say next for a laugh, followed by the deepest loneliness and depression I had felt since leaving the plane.

I followed the path back, and when emerging from the woods caught the merest glimpse of the creepy wee man that I had seen earlier, following me discreetly at some distance. Either he had been assigned to this duty, or he was doing so merely out of curiosity, or perhaps even boredom.

A little later, around midday, I sat at a table with the others in the house where I had eaten my first meal. Again it was soup..soup of a kind, this time minus the bread, with no one really acknowledging my presence, all being too busy devouring their own food. The noise and bustle of the place overwhelming, and I was glad when I had finished my frugal meal and gone out into the fresh air.

Once outside I walked to my ski lodge and sat down on one of the wooden steps, feeling utterly dismal and lonely, my mind whirling on what was happening to me, and how I could pass the time until Zofia arrived to take me away from this god forsaken place.

I sighed, shivering in the cool of the afternoon, at first unaware of the young woman passing carrying a box and a bundle of some sort. The box fell, and I ran down the steps to pick it up.

"Thank you." The woman was a few years younger than myself, not pretty, a face worn with worry and I guessed responsibility.

"Let me carry it," I smiled warmly at her, thankful to be doing something useful, or at least something to do to while away the time. She nodded and I walked beside her. "My name's West."

"Trudy," she said quietly.

"Pleased to meet you Trudy," I smiled broader.

"You are not hurt?" she asked with a certain amount of curiosity.

Puzzled by the question I answered, "No I am not hurt,"

"Then why should a foreigner be hunted by the government?"

"Now that's a question I should not care to answer."

"Sorry it was wrong for me to ask. It is not my business. Please do not let Arnau know that I asked the question."

She sounded worried and I hastened to assure her I would not.

We had reached the furthest building in the compound before she spoke again. "Thank you West, I can manage from here."

She made to take the box from me and I drew back a little. "Let me at least take it inside for you."

She thought for a moment before saying. "Okay but I must warn you, you might wish you had not."

She was right, on entering the building I wished I had not.

The place smelled of disinfectant amongst other smells I usually associated with hospitals.

The darkness of the room accentuated its gloominess. I put the box down, looking with some apprehension at the figures lying in a row of beds.

Trudy watched me stare. "They are... hurt, by our government. Tortured I think is the word, or in some cases, ill."

Only one sat up propped by a pillow, who gave me a weak pathetic wave, as if the presence of a new face had given him the will to live. In the far corner a solitary figure hovered by the side of one bed, who I guessed may be a doctor or some sort.

"Hello Trudy. Good, you have brought the supplies."

"Yes, Karl, Andrias brought them yesterday, when he brought West here with him," she answered in English.

"You are a doctor?" the figure asked hopefully, emerging out of the eerie semi darkness of the bedside.

"No, unfortunately." I answered, reluctant to approach closer, and wishing I had heeded Trudy's warning.

The doctor slit open the cardboard box. "It is as well that I do not immediately require any of these things, or I would be most cross with Andrias for not bringing them to me when he first arrived." The doctor bent to lift out a roll of bandages. "Is there nothing else?" he gave the box a slight kick. "It is morphine and antibiotics that I urgently require."

"No Karl that is all." She indicated the bundle she had carried when we first met. "These are clean bed sheets," her explanation having the good doctor turn away with a grunt.

I was only too happy to be outside once more, any longer inside and I would have thrown up at the sight of some of those poor devils the doctor had introduced me to. No doubt done to deliberately shock me, which it had done, and would no doubt have had the same affect on any healthy active person.

One, a leg amputated and his other I feared gangrenous, another, blind, lying still in his own silent lonely world. And so it had gone on.

The door opened. "You saw?" Trudy asked from where she stood on the top step.

I looked up at her. "Yes. How does he cope? Or more importantly how does his patients cope?" I splayed my hands. "How do they deal with all that pain?"

Trudy came down the steps. "They have no other choice. We do our best. It is a risk we all take when fighting for what we believe."

I did not want to ask what that might be, believing the less I knew about this country's politics the better.

Together we walked a little back to the main building.

"I will see you at supper time. I have a few more things to do."

I should have liked to have her company a bit longer, but I thought it prudent not to do so, besides I wanted another little walk amongst the trees to breathe in clean fresh air again. My depression having returned tenfold, and again I cursed my decision to ever having come on this accursed holiday turned nightmare.

I walked to the path leading into the woods and once again caught sight of my creepy wee shadow following me. I took the usual path all the while waiting for the man with the gun to step out from behind a tree and tell me in no uncertain terms not to come this way again, or so I believed that was what he had said last time.

It must have been a change of guard, for this time I was not halted when I walked further into the woods. At length I came to a small stream and sat down on a log to contemplate my position, still aware of my wee pal hiding in the background. Maybe I should introduce myself I thought, after all he could be a Hearts supporter who had got himself drunk and had taken the wrong turning after the game. If only, I sighed.

Chapter 5

Zofia did not arrive next day as I had hoped, so to cheer myself up I sought out Trudy. Only this time I waited until she had finished in the 'hospital' for want of a better word.

"Hello Trudy. I think it's going to be a nice day," Walking beside her I looked skywards.

She walked on. "It will rain later." She did not smile. "But you will be used to rain in your country, are you not?"

"It doesn't rain all of the time." I answered cheerfully, ready to make my old joke.

"No?"

"No," I said, "sometimes it snows."

She saw that I was making a joke and laughed. "Sometimes it snows," she echoed.

"Only in the summer of course," I added, attempting to keep the conversation light, "It's nice to hear you laugh."

My spirits lifted.

"Yes sometimes we laugh, mostly if we have enough vodka, then we sing and dance and forget our troubles for a little while." then she grew serious again, "Try to forget those we have left behind, husbands, wives, children."

"Yes that must be hard. Tell me Trudy why do I not see any children around?"

"This is not a place for children. Mostly those here have left their children with neighbours or family, but sometimes neighbours do not want to get involved."

I did not want to ask what happened to the children if this was the case.

"Sooner or later the army will find us, then it will no longer matter."

I looked at a face that appeared to carry all the sadness in the world. "Why are *you* here Trudy, or should I not ask?"

"My parents died when I was little. I was brought up by an uncle and aunt. I had a good job in a store. I did not mean to get involved in politics but could not ignore what was happening to honest people around me. Neighbours would suddenly disappear without any apparent reason. Eventually I was approached by a friend of Mark's who introduced me to his organisation." She shrugged, "That's how it all came about. I was betrayed and escaped to here. That was over two years ago."

"Two years!" I exclaimed, "in this place?"

"It is better than being dead, West. Besides, I get to help those who like myself are on the government hunted list."

I noted her choice of 'hunted' instead of 'wanted'. "Doesn't your uncle and aunt worry about you? Do they know where you are?"

"No, they do not worry. They are both dead. At their age they would not have survived long in one of our government's 'holiday resorts.' " She halted. "I must go in here and help the women. I will see you later."

I mumbled yes and watched her leave. A few days ago I knew nothing of this place or these people, all leading lives far from that of my own, existing in a parallel universe, one which I could no longer ignore or switch off as you would a TV set. A world only a few hours away by plane but a thousand miles away in culture and I was thankful for my own country, some like me who moaned and groaned at almost everything, never stopping to think how lucky we were at having the freedom to moan and groan at all.

It was time for my afternoon walk, and for the hundredth time glanced at my wrist where my watch should have been. "Damn you Sowa," I said aloud and walked to the trees.

Another day and still no sign of Zofia. Was it Mark's intention to leave me here to rot, or until he found it convenient to have me moved, or worse still, *removed.*

I stepped down into the compound, yawned and took my first look up at the morning sky. It looked like rain, of which I was hopeful as the heat of the day even way up here in the mountains was oppressive.

On the other side of the compound Trudy was running to the building that could vaguely be called a hospital. On impulse I started after her. In her haste she had left the door open and I hurried inside, convinced something was wrong.

I was right. At the far end of the room the doctor was in the act of dragging a body along the floor. Trudy had an arm around a moaning patient sitting up in bed, she was doing her best to comfort him.

The doctor looked up, saw me, and halted in what he was doing. "Can you give me a hand please?"

Very reluctantly I took a few steps forward.

"He took his own life…. couldn't take any more. Can't say I blame him."

I looked down to where the doctor still held the arms of the dead man. It was the one with the gangrenous leg.

I swallowed but tried not to breathe too deeply as if afraid to be contaminated by the dead man.

"Take one of his hands." the doctor had lost patience with my reluctance.

I stepped over the body but not the thick pool of blood under the corpse and grasped the still warm hand, and helped drag the body to the side of the room.

The doctor let go of the dead man's hand and I did the same.

"I'll get two of the men to help bury him in the woods." He wiped his hands. "Thanks for the help."

Trudy released herself from her patient's hold, a young man no more than eighteen I should say.

I knew by her look that she intended to clear up the mess on the floor. Without thinking, I said, "I'll do that. Where can I find a mop or something?"

"Outside, West."

"Good."

I found a mop standing in a pail just outside the door, and filled the pail from a tap next to it.

Trudy was laying down her young patient in the bed talking softly to him and covering him with the coarse grey blanket that was uniform in what stood for a hospital.

I started to mop up the blood. Trudy stopped what she was doing to watch.

"Pity it's not hot water," I said, dipping the bloody mop into the pail. It was not a grey bucket that usually went with mopping, just an ordinary pail so I had to go back outside and hold the mop under the tap to wash it clean.

On my way back up the steps I met the doctor. "I'll get two men to come and take Mercus away, poor soul. I don't know how his wife will take it." He pushed past me. "Bloody war."

Pail in hand I went back inside. There was still blood on the floor, and I mopped at the dark patch. Now the surrounding area looked dirty. It was similar at having decided to paint something to freshen it up, only to discover that what you were painting made the rest look shabby, so you just kept going until it was all done. It was the same here, I just kept on mopping and washing and drying until the entire room was finished.

Trudy had sat on the edge of the bed watching me. Eventually when I had done she walked to where I stood leaning on my mop.

"You have done well," her smile one of amusement, "Would you like a job here?"

"Not on your life, or anyone else's for that matter." I answered seriously, "How you cope each and every day is beyond me, Trudy."

"If not me someone else," She lifted the pail, "Come on let's have a coffee you deserve one."

That same night I decided to take a walk in the pale moonlight with half a hope that Trudy might join me. She did not. My wee shadow watched me from the corner of a building. Was he a half wit, or even a football supporter, either would explain his actions?

That he meant me no harm was plain having had several opportunities to have done just that. Perhaps it was only idle curiosity. I walked on, reaching the corner of the main building when I heard the music. At first I was startled by the unexpected sound, and above all the laughter from within.

Curious, on tip toe I peered in a window, at the couples dancing and laughing as their partners swung them round, those watching, clapping or swinging their drinks in time to the music of the accordion player.

I stepped back, the contrast too much for me to comprehend after the day's events.

The door opened and a big man came out and stood on the top step. He saw me standing in the shadows, and swaying, cheerfully held out his half empty bottle of vodka to me.

At first my intention was to refuse his kind offer until I saw his expression change. Obviously it was not considered good manners to refuse a drink when offered; something similar to home except here good Samaritans carried foot long knives in their belts whereas at home? I thought again well at least not in the East they didn't, well maybe just one or two did when their team lost.

I trotted up the steps and grinning took the bottle from him, swigging back a mouthful and handing it back with a wink and a thanks. In return he slapped me heavily on the back in a gesture I hoped was in friendship, not relishing what he would do to me if not.

It was hot inside, and I unobtrusively took up a position against the wall, watching the women dancers swirl while their partners stomped, slapped their thighs, and chest and other parts of their anatomy.

"You like our dancing?" It was Trudy who had spoken.

It was the first time I had seen her in a frock. I was stunned at the transformation. I choked, "So you found me? You look lovely Trudy."

She blushed and held out a glass of vodka in a far from steady hand. "Thank you, kind sir," she tittered.

I took the glass from her. "I believe you're a bit tipsy, Trudy."

"Tipsy? What is tipsy?" she took an unsteady step towards me.

Another step I thought and she will be in my arms. "Tipsy? It means a bit drunk."

I waited for her next step, which to my disappointment was backwards.

"Come you will dance with me," Trudy commanded, grasping my hand and dragging me on to the floor.

In horror I saw what I was supposed to do, lift my leg and slap the sole of my shoe..or in their case, boot, and squat while thumping my thigh.

"You do this in your country?" Trudy laughed.

"Only when fighting off the midgies."

"Midgies? What are midgies?"

"Wee nuisances," I replied, "They come from deepest Amazon on holiday." Anything else that I was about to add was terminated by someone grabbing my would be partner and swinging her in amongst the swirling dancers.

Sighing in relief I edged my way back amongst the onlookers while watching Trudy appear and reappear amongst the spinning, happy throng.

"You enjoy?" I turned to face Arnau. "It is just like home eh?"

"Yes. Something, like home." And to myself, *the noise was the same, and you had to shout just as loud to make yourself heard.*

Arnau guided me to a long table, lifted a vodka bottle and filled a generous measure into a glass. "You did very good work today." He handed me the brimming glass, then filled his own.

"I mean cleaning the hospital, no?"

I shrugged that it was nothing, thinking hospital was not a word I would have used. Then again, what else did these poor buggers have?

"It was for the best, what the doctor did."

"But the doctor said that he took his own life, that he couldn't take the pain any more."

I stared at the leader my drink forgotten.

Arnau twisted his lip a little. "It is best it is thought that was what happened."

I felt a cold sweat sweep through me and took a shaky gulp of my drink, not wanting to hear any more.

The burly man glared at me having seen my change of expression. "It was best, Crom pleaded that it should be done. There was no hope..only pain for him You understand?"

He waved a hand at the dancers. "This is for Crom..it is…how you say farewell?"

"A wake," I explained.

"Ah! A wake," he nodded digesting the word.

"Is it also your custom not to have anyone attend the funeral?" I was angry now, the vodka had filled me with Dutch courage.

Arnau matched my anger. "There is enough sadness here without weeping at a graveside."

Again he waved a hand at the merriment. "This is how we grieve. And should you have taken the time my Mr West, you would also have seen how many other graves were there."

I do not remember much more of the remainder of the evening, only that at one stage I was violently sick outside. Vaguely, through a film of fog, or was it vodka, Trudy holding me in her arms as I sat on the bottom step, and I unsuccessfully tried to kiss her.

Also a continual echo inside my head at her telling me how much I had angered Arnau, and that I should be wary of him from now on.

Why did two bands have to play at the same time and both out of tune? One a pipe band the other, what sounded like a steel calypso band each playing a different tune. I lay on my bunk moaning, promising never to indulge in alcohol again. I closed my eyes having given up on life and deciding to die, and if this racket inside my head did not stop, the sooner the better.

No. It was no use. I had to get up, get some fresh air. Delicately I swung my legs out of bed and more delicately the rest of my body followed.

My head in my hands I sat there for what must have been a year or two, perhaps longer. Thirsty, I ran my tongue round my lips, or what I believed to be my tongue but just as easily could have been a sheet of sandpaper.

At the third attempt having succeeded on putting on my shoes I staggered to the door, and with a little more staggering reached the foot of the steps. The cold air hit me and I shivered, shivering even more as I doused my head under the cold water tap.

Someone passed wishing me what I understood to be a good morning or perhaps it was 'numpty' in their language.

My ablutions complete I sat down shakily on the bottom step. *Please God that Zofia did not call for me today, as the last thing I wanted was a long car journey, especially over these roads.*

Eventually I rose and made my way to the main building, now in desperate need of a cup of coffee, but should anyone offer me anything to eat, murder would be done.

In contrast to the previous night, the place was silent, except when someone let a tin plate drop and my head rang like a bell on a fire engine with the reverberations.

There must have been over a dozen or so women cleaning up last night's mess, and I was forced to get out of there before the continual clinking of empty vodka bottles the clanging of tin mugs and plates had me commit a serious international incident.

Suddenly it came to me, and I wish it hadn't, I needed the toilet. I ran…well as best as I could without crossing my legs, back to my cabin, fumbling open my backpack for my book, and tearing out a few pages, desperation dulling the thought of what those outside that stood for toilets were like.

Relieved in more ways than one when I had finished, though in a way sad at what I had done to my book, and apologising to the author that it was in no way a reflection of his work, I headed for the silence of the woods, but with my luck a flock of squawking birds would have gathered for their annual get together to elect their new leader, and little furry creatures would scurry pass wearing wooden clogs, as I sat there once more contemplating passing away. Thinking should this be so, and my neighbours here decided to cremate me the explosion from what was left of my internal alcohol would knock out half of them and alert Sowa as to where I was or had been. My stupid fantasies over I instantly fell asleep.

At first when I awoke, I did not understand where I was. Then it came slowly back to me. I was sitting on the grass, my back against a tall tree. I yawned, licked my dry lips and took in a deep breath. I would sit a little until the return of my faculties, or maybe not all of them, for now I felt ravenously hungry.

I rose awkwardly, reluctant to let go of my friendly tree. I scanned around. This was not my usual walk. I focused my eyes in one direction struggling to recognise anything that would give me a clue as to where I was, and cursed at my wee shadow not being there as usual.

I kicked my legs into circulation and succeeding, I felt happy enough to find my way back to camp.

It was as I took a few steps away from my tree that I heard the snap of a twig. My wee shadow at last had come to help me.

I swung round, this was not my wee shadow or if he was, he had suddenly grown a foot or two, and the blade that glinted in his hand, as was this giant not too friendly.

His momentum carried him to me and he lunged at me with the knife.

A few minutes earlier this assassin would have caught me asleep. I had seen him in the camp, but had never spoken to him. Why did he want to kill me? Or why should anyone want to?

I parried the blow and swung my fist which only caught him partially on the chin.

It did nothing to hinder the killer.

Adrenaline pumping now that I was forced to fight for my life I hit him again as he swung round, and although his knife narrowly missed me, he had succeeded in clutching my jacket and hitting me midriff. I yelped at the blow, and he pulled me to him, one hand at my throat the other ready to stab at my chest. I did what I had been to taught to do by big brother Fenton when I and been bullied at school, I kneed him in the goolies. Moaning he staggered back giving me sufficient time to follow with another punch.

Now incensed, no doubt by my lack of fair play head down he charged at me and I felt myself lifted off my feet and hurtled against a tree. Stunned, my unfocused eyes were on a figure standing over me his knife ready to deliver the coup de grace. It was all over. My brain flashed to my brother, and our lives. This the end, in this God forsaken place?

I fought to rise, determined not to let this animal end it, I glared hatred and anger at him as the knife flashed down towards me. I closed my eyes waiting for the pain and the end. Then an unexpected weight on my chest and I opened my eyes to my attacker sprawled across me a knife protruding from the middle of his back and a wee man grinning down at me.

"What kept you?" was all I could think of to say, and I almost blacked out with the shock. And to damn it all my headache was back.

Instantly it seemed there were people all around. One I recognised as Arnau, lifting the dead man off my chest, another helping me to my feet.

Now that the shock was setting in I was growing angry at everything and everyone. I wanted to walk away, get out of there, get out of this place, this country.

"You are all right mister West?" Arnau asked, using my first same.

"What the hell is going on? That mongrel tried to kill me." I took an angry step towards him, staring him in the face. "You're the leader here, so tell me why."

Arnau looked around him. "Perhaps this is not the best place, Eh" he snapped his fingers at a man, pointing down at my late assailant. Then back at me, "Come we will speak in my place."

My anger kept me from losing my balance as I followed the burly man. Then a little way out of the woods I caught sight of Trudy, she looked pale, trembling a little as she met me.

"You are not hurt, West?" her eyes swept over me.

"No, only my feelings. What's it all about Trudy?"

She did not answer, instead she turned away. "Arnau will explain it all. You are safe now."

Safe! What the hell did that mean?

Together with my little life saver and someone else I did not know, Arnau led the way to his quarters where he proceeded to pour each of us a drink, and gestured that I sit down.

"We have been watching the man who attacked you, long before you came here," he explained. "We believed him to be a spy, but could never actually prove it, that is until you came along. We had him believe that you were a Mr Malcolm, the man who had come to help us."

Arnau halted at the hostility in my eyes. "You set me up," I seethed.

"It was the only way, my friend."

"The only way!" I shouted. "You could at least have had the decency to let me know what was going on, given me a chance to be on the look out to defend myself." I stammered angrily.

"Perhaps. But what if you gave yourself away? What then? You could have been in even more danger."

Arnau took a sip of his drink. I took a gulp.

"Besides you were well guarded by Jesic here, who watched you every day." The little man grinned at the mention of his name, though I guessed he did not understand a word that was said. "That is until today when you decided to take a different path." Arnau wagged a finger at me. "That was most naughty." He ventured a smile which I did not return.

"Look, pal I don't know what all this is about and don't want to. All I know is that I'm here until a certain young lady comes to pick me up and whisk me back to my own country via Poland. Okay."

"This I understand. But at least you can say that you helped us in our cause. Yes?"

Arnau was trying to make amends, but in no way to apologise at having used me. And sipping my drink I tried hard not to let him see me shake as the reaction of how close I had come to having a knife tear through my gut.

"Zofia will be here early tomorrow morning, until then the time is yours. Use it as you will. But please remember what happened to you today happened to us and our friends which is why we are here in the first place, and for how much longer we do not know. What you did a little time ago may just have helped to shorten our stay that little bit."

It proved to be an awkward evening, Arnau kept well away from me, my little rescuer lifting his drink to me in salute as I sat at a corner table, others acknowledging me with a smile as they passed.

Eventually Trudy slid onto a bench opposite me. "You are leaving tomorrow." It was not a question but a statement.

I lifted my drink. "I sincerely hope so."

"You do not like it here?" She sounded hurt.

"No I do not," I replied angrily. "In fact I don't like any of your damned country."

It was an offensive thing to say, but considering how close I had come to being here forever, albeit six feet under, I felt justified.

"You want to be in your own country where everybody is safe, not here where people have to hide when they are not. Easy for you to say, Mr West Barns." She was angry now and I must admit justifiably so. "Your country is very beautiful so I am told?"

I nodded. Seeing the lochs and mountains again.

"So is ours but we do not have... how you say the luxury to enjoy it. That is why we must fight."

"I understand," I apologised.

"No you do not and never will, West, not until it happens to you. Never to go where and when you want. The right to protest at the price of bread without being taken away, having no work, or if you do, it is to find that all the best jobs are held by those friendly to our government."

I held up my hands in surrender, annoyed by what she was telling me. "Okay so you and these folk here," I waved a hand around me, "are having a hard time, so are folk in many other countries. However you forget I never wanted to be here in the first place. All I really wanted was a few days holiday in Poland." Again I waved a hand around. "And with all due respect this is hardly what I would call a holiday camp."

For a moment there was a glimmer of a smile, and I decided to go for it. "Trudy, this is my last night here, cannot we at least be friends?" I gave her my best *'I'm really a nice guy'* smile. Well, it had worked with some other girls.

She studied what I had said for a moment. "Okay. We will drink to our friendship and your sad leaving."

I laughed, "I will drink to that," Remembering my hangover, I added, "But not too much." And Trudy laughed with me.

That night I hardly slept, so excited I was at the prospect of leaving this place, though I felt strangely disturbed at leaving Trudy behind, not out of any amorous feelings as such, but more out of some sort of guilt. Hopefully this time I would make it home, and safe again or relatively so in North Berwick while she would still be here in this dismal god forsaken place.

Again I thought of that night's conversation on how I like many of my countrymen took what we had for granted. Of how we would cope in a similar situation lasting for days, months on end, never knowing how and when it was all going to end?

Yes I thought we take a lot for granted. Now more than ever I wanted to put this nightmare behind me.

Chapter 6

Zofia appeared around 7 am. I had been up from 5. She saw me walking, running almost to meet her.

"So you have survived, West, I see," she greeted me with a kiss on the cheek and it took all of my willpower not to hug her to death.

"Just. Any longer and it would have been a wasted journey," I beamed, unable to express my happiness at my leaving at last.

We walked away from her car that was being eagerly unpacked of supplies, mostly I saw of the medical variety.

I sat at a table in the main building while Arnau and Zofia discussed what no doubt was group business etc. At last she rose, uttering the words I so longed to hear. "Time to go, West."

We walked to the door and down the steps. "Do you have everything?" she asked.

I held up my backpack. "All that I possess."

Arnau's handshake was short of warm. "Look after yourself, Mr West Barns."

I nodded that I would. Trudy kissed me on the cheek, whispering before she stepped back, "we might meet again someday when things are better."

I thought, perhaps, but I was in no hurry, even it was to meet her again. Then we were off to the border and so to home.

Zofia was the first to break the silence. "Was it bad?"

I knew what she meant. I stared out of the window. "Not an experience I would care to repeat."

"At least you were safe, safe that is, until we try and cross the border."

My silence had her take a swift look at me. So, I thought Arnau had not told her of the little 'Mr Malcolm incident.' All I said was, "I suppose so." Perhaps when the time was right I might tell her, but for now just let's be on our way.

It was early afternoon before we left the mountains behind, gradually descending to more peaceful green pastures.

"We shall stop and have a bite to eat. You are hungry?" Zofia drew the car to a halt on the side of a single track road. She got out, "You will find coffee and some bread in that basket." Zofia pointed to the back seat from where she stood at the door. "I am going over there behind that bush. You can do the same when I return."

"Thanks." I swivelled around and lifted the basket, a little put out by Zofia's lack of warmth to me, maybe she would after she had had a pee. Then again she could just be tired, after all it was a long way from Mark's house to here.

We started on our way and to help pass the time, I asked, "I suppose Mark would have liked to have left me there?"

"It did occur to him, but Serge talked him out of it, as did Andrias."

"Nice to know I still have friends."

Zofia scowled at me. "They did it out of necessity not friendship, Mr West Barns, believe me."

I said nothing more, not wishing to hear what might have been in store for me had those two guys agreed with their leader. Then again it left me wondering why I should be so important when it was easier to leave me lying in some country bog.

Once again when on our way I asked. "Where are we actually going, Zofia?"

"To a town from where we shall take a train towards the coast. Then another train over the border."

"So although it's the coast, I'm not going by boat?"

"No."

As a landlubber I heaved a sigh of relief. North Berwick might lie by the sea but my only interest was looking out of my office window to ensure the Bass Rock was still afloat. I sat back and closed my eyes. Perhaps this time things would work out all right.

It was late when we reached the town, and although tired Zofia had not trusted me to drive on the right side of the road in a left hand drive, I had left her to it and fell asleep for most of the way.

She chose a reasonable decent looking hotel, introducing me to the receptionist as her fiancé, a deaf mute. I played the part well, smiling in a way that suggested I could lip read.

Once alone in the elevator Zofia suddenly broke into laughter. Mystified I stared at her, she not having as much as raised a smile for most of the journey.

"What's so funny?" I drew her a look.

"You," she laughed again. "I said that you could lip read. All we needed was the receptionist to say, that she understood sign language, and…"

"I would be well and truly buggered," I grinned.

We shared the one room as expected of an engaged couple. Zofia delved into her holdall extracting a plastic container. "I made these this morning, this is our supper." She pointed to an electric kettle standing on a small table in the corner. "You can make some coffee whilst I shower." She pulled a few clothes out of her bag, and disappeared into the bathroom.

By the time I had made coffee from the usual little paper sachets, Zofia had finished her toilet. A towel round her head and one covering her upper body she lifted a cup of coffee and sipped it. "No sugar," she complained.

"I didn't know whether you took any or not." I handed her a white tube.

I took a drink of mine. "Can I have one of your sandwiches before I shower, I'm a bit peckish?"

"Peckish? What are you, a bird?"

"No you're a bird." She looked puzzled so I explained what a bird meant in our language, thinking how stupid a term it was, the same I thought as calling a full grown woman baby.

When I had devoured a sandwich and gulped down a coffee, I took out my toiletries bag together with a body spray and my one and only clean shirt, clean because I had washed it way back at Mark's and again when holidaying in my mountain retreat.

I saw Zofia watching me, and I explained, "This is all that thief Sowa left me." I held up the articles for her inspection.

"That is all?"

I pulled out my wee novel. "No, this as well. I think Sowa must have read it so left it. I'm so glad he didn't tell me the ending," I chuckled.

"You are so strange, West Barns. Are all Scotchmen like you?"

I scratched my head. "No some are even stranger, taller too."

"They all wear…" she ran her hands over the bottom of her towel, "skirts?"

I pretended to be aghast. "Skirts are worn by women, men wear kilts."

She laughed, "How would I know the difference?"

"Oh you would soon know," I chuckled, "somehow I think you would soon know." I turned for the bathroom and my shower.

When I returned Zofia was sitting on the edge of the bed studying what appeared to be a train timetable.

"Have you figured it out?" I asked having decided to re heat the kettle and have another coffee.

"I think so." She did not take her eyes off the pamphlet. "First we leave the car in the next town. Then we will take two trains, one almost to the coast."

I sat down in a chair across from her, my eyes on her legs bare to the knee. I swallowed and brought my thoughts back to the business in hand. "You will not be coming with me all the way?"

"No once you are safely on the second train I will return for my car."

I nodded. "Will you go straight back home? Or will you stop over at my mountain lodge?"

She took her eyes off the pamphlet and smiled across at me at my humour.

"No, I shall go straight home. It will mean driving most of the night, but I cannot be away from work too long, you understand."

Yawning Zofia put the timetable down. "You still have your Polish passport, and the money Mark gave you for your last trip?"

"Yes, let's hope this one will be more successful. How many know of my attempt this time?"

Zofia looked annoyed. "You think there is someone in our organisation that is a spy?"

"Could be. They were waiting for me last time."

"And one lost his life." Zofia said bitterly.

"Then why don't you leave me to my own devices before anyone else dies?" I countered.

"Can't do that West Barns it is too late, you know too much to be caught." She swung round to face me. "And God help us all if you are."

Zofia stood up, walked to a row of shelves and took down three pillows. "What side do you wish to sleep?" She threw the pillows down the centre of the double bed.

I rose. "This side will do, but I must warn you lady, I usually sleep alone, so there's no accounting at what I might do, snore, kick."

"If that is all you intend doing I can cope, anything else and you will find I too can snore and kick, mainly kick. Okay?"

Though tired I did not immediately fall asleep, my thoughts on why I should be so important. I could well see that if captured I might give the game away. I knew too much, much easier to just give me a bullet. I did not wholly believe that Mark's reason for helping me was in return for my having been taken for the mysterious Mr Malcolm and therefore obligated in trying to get me back across the border. No, there was more to it than that. Of one thing I was certain, Zofia would make sure that I was never taken alive.

I turned on to my back. Beside me I heard Zofia's deep breathing. I stared up at the ceiling. She must have a gun, and my bet was that she would use it if she thought I was about to be captured.

I lay there. I must get the gun, for the lady next to me would have no hesitation in using it, there were too many involved should I decide to 'grass' as the saying goes, about everything and everyone I knew. After all it was not my war.

I waited until convinced that Zofia was indeed asleep. I slid one leg out of bed, several heart beats later the other, deliriously happy that I was not a centipede. I raised the rest of me out of bed, cursing softly at a twang of a bedspring.

The room was in semi darkness in the summer's night, the only light an occasional flash of a cars headlights from the street below. I moved to my room-mate's side of the bed where her bag lay, my eyes never leaving the sleeping form for any sign of movement.

I knelt down drew the bag closer and quietly rummaged through it for the familiar feel of a weapon.

"You won't find it there, West, it's under my pillow," my companion said without moving. "Now go back to bed."

After breakfast we made our way to the rail station, Zofia left me sitting on one of benches with the final warning to look dumb, *no trouble there I thought, and to try and not jump at the merest unexpected sound.*

Soon tickets in hand she was back.

"Okay? No trouble?" she asked sliding down next to me.

I mumbled 'No'.

"Our train will leave in about fifteen minutes. I got tickets for its destination, but we will get off two stops before that just in case anyone is on the lookout for us. We'll swap trains for another one going closer to the border."

"Clever." I said admiringly.

"You soon learn in my way of life," she glanced at her watch, "Give it another five minutes then we will saunter to the gate."

We got on board without difficulty raising my hopes that the second train would be as equally easy. Also having no one sitting next to us helped to ease both our tensions.

However that was short lived when a rather overweight lady and her little girl sat down beside us. The lady smiled at us saying something to Zofia while the little girl stared at me, *must be a relative of the one on the plane I thought.* Then again, that one on the plane would be all grown up by now, and no doubt have a family in the time I had been in this country, or so it seemed.

A little while later the lady leaned forward and offered me what looked like chocolate cake, wrapped in tin foil urging me to take a slice, and looking a little upset at my silence, until Zofia came to my rescue.

In a moment all was transformed, the lady nodding knowingly and offering me a sympathetic smile, the little girl's eyes opening even wider in wonder.

I took a piece, smiling and nodding my appreciation, quite happy at my performance, this and the vision of me onstage at the next Oscars receiving my award and delivering the best acceptance speech ever. *Until then, just keep dreaming and chewing son.*

Next stop they were gone, the wee lassie with a final cheery wave.

Due to Zofia's caution by changing trains we alighted at the next station.

Upon reaching the forecourt Zofia again left me as she purchased the tickets.

I took a sly look around me at the hustle and bustle of ordinary folk going about their business the only difference to any other station in the world, the high profile of patrolling armed police. Swiftly I stared down at my feet ensuring non eye contact with anyone likely to look my way, appealing Zofia to hurry.

A few minutes later she was back, sitting close beside me, and sliding my rail ticket into my hand.

"Should we by chance get separated before you get on your train, remember your role."

She stopped for a moment, before continuing, "you have money and your passport?"

I gave a slight nod.

"The train will not stop until it reaches the border, guards will already be on board and will ask to see your passport. Don't panic; take your time to convince them you are in fact a deaf mute."

"Mutt," I murmured softly to myself.

Zofia glanced at her watch. "Your train will come in at platform five. I will leave you and hope you get home safely and..." Zofia swore, her face void of colour. "Leave, sit somewhere else," she said hurriedly, her voice suddenly filled with fear and panic. "Don't worry about me just get on your train."

At first stunned by Zofia's sudden change I looked to where a young man was walking towards us calling out her name, and by his look of surprise someone whom he had never expected to see here.

I rose as casually as I could, to give the impression I was not with this woman that this young man clearly knew.

Finding a seat a little away, I watched the two greet one another, then appearing to say goodbye Zofia walked quickly away, passing where I sat without as much as a glance in my direction, followed almost immediately by her new acquaintance.

The station clock said that I had ten minutes before my trains departure. I swore softly to myself. Zofia was clearly in trouble. I sat there watching her walk to the foot of the elevator, the young man not so far behind.

My eyes left her to the gate leading to my platform, so close and yet so far, all I had to do was show my ticket and walk to my train. So what was stopping me? Was this not what Zofia, Mark and the others had worked for, to have me safely home?

Now Zofia was on the elevator, her stalker only a few strides behind.

Even before I knew what I was doing I was running, running amongst a few others late for their train. Zofia was on the bridge now, the man grabbing her shoulder and turning her around. She saw me, her face showing anger and frustration at my being there, but still grappling with the man who refused to release his hold.

I came at him from behind pushing him none too gently against the rail, Zofia on his other side pushing up against his body. The man shouted something, struggling to free himself, suddenly the tannoy sounded, the man jerked, went limp, and I wrapped an arm around him to prevent him from falling.

Aware of passers-by staring at us we held him bent over against the rail as if he was about to vomit on the trains below, Zofia thrusting the small pistol she had used into her coat pocket.

"Go! You can still make your train!" she hurled at me.

"And you? What about you?" I leaned harder on the sagging figure.

"Never mind me, just go!"

We were attracting too much attention. A few drew closer, their curiosity aroused.

I let him go and ran back the way I had come seeking out the 'down' escalator, aware of Zofia running in the opposite direction, and of screams from the bridge, obviously having found our man dead.

As a man running late for his train I ran towards the still open gate of my platform, ticket at the ready. Gasping for breath I handed the collector my ticket, hearing a voice that I thought familiar saying, "You won't be requiring that Mr Barns, I can assure you," and I was looking into the sneering face of a certain Captain Sowa.

Chapter 7

It was a cellar, a dark cellar. What scared the life out of me was the screaming naked man hanging by the wrists in the far corner.

"You would not care for the same treatment, Mr Barns?" The smoke from Sowa's cheroot rose lazily to the black stone roof.

A further scream had me shiver and I wrenched my eyes away from the bleeding form.

"So tell me Mr Scotchman where have you been hiding since we last met?"

I swallowed. "Here and there. Mostly there."

"Not so very funny my friend. Please do not waste my time."

"Why, can't your little racket survive without you?" I bit back.

Sowa sighed pretending to be bored. "We have room for one more over there you know," Sowa pointed to the hanging man. He gave a nod and a heavily built man ran a hot iron over the tortured man's back.

I gulped, attempting not to show my fear. The unfortunate man's additional suffering was for my benefit.

"So I shall ask you once again. Where have you been and with whom since you were rescued that first day of your arrival?"

I stared at Sowa. "I wouldn't have a clue. I don't even know who *they* were or what *they* wanted."

"You think me a half wit Barns?"

"You flatter yourself Sowa. Let me ask *you* something, what brings you, or should I say who brings you to this part of the country? I know it could not be your intelligence."

By the look of sheer anger on the policeman's face I feared that I may have gone too far and could shortly be hanging next to the room's occupant.

"That my friend is none of your business. However what is my business is you telling me where you have been since your lucky escape by the hands of terrorists."

I had to think fast. The torturer seemed a bit too keen to ply his trade on me. I had always had a low pain threshold, even lower at seeing what this moron had done to the poor sod hanging there, and I had a notion both he and Sowa would find it interesting how I would stand up to their form of persuasion.

"You know the papers are aware of my disappearance," I started, but afraid that my voice was betraying my fear. "Also my brother, who is with the police force back home, and not without influence, will not rest until he finds me and I am returned to Poland." Out of fear I had made it sound as though I was a mislaid parcel.

Sowa clearly was not swayed by any manner of means. "You are wasting my time, Barns, pleased to have you undress, and we will find out the truth," he pointed to the suffering man, "And for your own sake, before you look like that."

Fear and anger made me resist. "You better make a good job of it, Sowa. Any attempt to return me like a roasted pig will have a few people asking the reason, which in turn might have them asking about your little enterprise."

For a moment Sowa hesitated, raising my hopes, but only fractionally. "Who is to say it was me who had done this dreadful thing to you? After all you were only in my care for a little time before you were rescued. My detaining you was perfectly legal, you being in possession of drugs." Sowa grinned triumphantly knowing he had bested me. "So strip! I want to know where and who you were with!"

I was not too keen on being tortured for someone else's beliefs, what was going on in this country was of no concern of mine, and should I have to name names so be it. Fractionally but only fractionally Trudy's face leaped before me at my intended betrayal.

"What do you want to know Sowa?" My question was little more than a frightened whisper.

Sowa beamed at me. "Now you are being sensible Mr Barns." He signalled to one of the guards to take me upstairs.

I choked relief. At least I had escaped the unpleasantness of torture for the present.

I was sat none too gently on a chair facing across a small table from the man himself, in a small, but after the bestiality of the cellar, dull but otherwise acceptable room.

I sat there while Sowa took his time in rummaging through my backpack, extracting besides my toiletries, clothes, what was left of my book and last of all my train ticket.

"You have dual nationality I see," Sowa laughed holding up my Polish passport. "Of course it is a forgery. One other crime you have committed in my country. No doubt you will tell me how you came by it."

"I needed it to get out of your wonderful country after you stole mine." I sounded tired, but I was not going to give in to this moron, and hopefully I still had an ace or two to play. The trouble was how many had this man up his sleeve?

"Perhaps you can begin by telling the names of those who have helped you?"

I shrugged. "I was never given names, and those that I do know are probably not their real ones."

"Let me be the judge of that." Sowa flicked a hand at a soldier sitting notebook in hand.

"First tell me where you were taken after your escape."

"I was driven to a farmhouse somewhere off a dirt road. Don't ask me where. I had only just arrived in your country you will remember." I added sarcastically.

Sowa snapped his fingers impatiently."Yes! yes! We know all that."

I shrugged again. "Sorry. I didn't know that," I lied.

"This farmhouse, it was the one we raided and had to shoot the old woman when she resisted. You were lucky to escape, Barns."

Resisted, I thought, pull the other one.

"Where were you taken? What town was it?"

"I don't know, they put a hood over my head. I neither saw the town or the house they took me to, all I know is that it was a big house." *Lie number one I thought.*

"How long would you say were you in the car from leaving the farmhouse?"

It was another officer who had asked the question, and his captain did not look at all pleased.

"I couldn't really say, I fell asleep after awhile." I stared at both officers in turn. "It was a long protracted flight, after all. We were supposed to touchdown at Krakow, so it's no wonder I fell asleep, I was knackered."

Both men looked at one another puzzled by the word, and I was not about to explain it to them.

"But you did see the driver? There were more than two that freed you from my station."

"Only briefly. One was a girl, well a young woman in her twenties, quite good looking with dark brown hair. That was before they put my hood on."

"Surely you met the owner of this big house," the junior officer asked with a slight glance at his superior for approval.

"No. Same there." I pointed to my head, "hood still on." *Lie number two.* "They took me to a room, locked the door, fed me and let me out to the bathroom when it was their turn to wear a mask."

I sat back in my chair feeling a little more at ease, together with a wee bit pleasure at the look of annoyance on Sowa's face at my lack of description.

"How long were you kept there, Barns."

I pretended to consider the question. "Could have been a week, perhaps longer." *Lie number three.* As I was on my second attempt to cross the border by that time, I could not extend the time. "They, whoever they were, attempted to get me over the border. Obviously they did not succeed, and one of their men was shot dead, or so I believe."

"Then what happened? Where did you go from there?"

This I should have to work out, any anomalies to my answer could well put all and what else I might say up the spout, or words similar to it.

"I ran back to where the driver had parked the car. He had managed to escape. However about an hour later," *Lie number four. It was closer to two hours, but I had to put them off trying to work out the distance from Mark's house to the railway station.* "he stopped the car and made me wear the hood again, then took me back to the big house and the same room and procedure." I sighed. "All quite boring, you'll agree." The latter I thought was quite a nice touch as used in some of the old English pictures.

Sowa lit up another cheroot watched the smoke drift lazily to the far from clean ceiling, then back to me. "Tell me Barns, why did these terrorists go to such lengths to try and get you back to Poland? What lies do you possess that they want the world to know about Eh? Perhaps I might not be dealing with a drug dealer but instead a spy? What do you say Mr Scotchman?"

"Think what you like Sowa. The papers are aware that I was arrested by you for my alleged drug possession. Also I believe that by this time my brother will be creating hell with various police forces to have me released."

"All very convincing my friend, but it fails to answer the question of why terrorists should risk their lives in trying to smuggle you across the border, if as you say you are of no importance to them?"

I had no more time to think, therefore I had to get this part right. "They mistook me for someone else. When they discovered their mistake they thought it only right that they should help me get back to Poland which I couldn't do without a passport. Also having already been arrested for drug possession by an overzealous policeman, it made it even more difficult." The latter I added sarcastically.

I breathed relief at Sowa's expression, which seemed to say that he believed my story. After all it was close to the truth even although some of the rest of my story was not. However I could be mistaken, and still find myself hanging beside the unfortunate man down in the cellar.

Sowa rose abruptly, speaking to his junior officer. "Take him to Zatvor, let him sweat for a time amongst some of our most distinguished guests."

I almost dropped dead with fear. I might have escaped one form of torture for another, for I had no doubt Sowa's intention was to scare the truth out of me if not physically but mentally by incarcerating me with this prisons worse offenders.

"You may take your bag," Sowa held up the passport "but without this of course, which will be evidence at your trial."

I scooped up the few things remaining to me which I would no doubt lose upon reaching this notorious prison, into my backpack, and hoped Zofia and her mob would do a repeat performance by rescuing me once again.

However it was not to be. Besides, I told myself Zofia, should she herself have evaded capture, know where I was being held?

I was again bundled into a car. This journey would no doubt take some time should I be returning to the prison close to the border where I was first arrested. Was it possible that in that time, Mark, Serge or Andrias might hear of my arrest and come to my rescue, fearing that I might spill my guts so to speak, or should that be vomit?

Handcuffed, I sat in the back there were two young police officers in the front. From the start they played the radio loud and non stop, until my head was splitting. I must be growing old I thought. I sat back working out my next move, that's should I have one.

One thing was clear I was not going to be locked up amongst perverts rapists and every other conceivable scum known to man and dog for that matter, therefore my best chance of avoiding this was to attempt an escape from here, from this car.

Fortunately I was not handcuffed with my hands behind me, so I sat there with my backpack on my lap.

One of policemen threw a bottle of water over his shoulder for me to catch, saying something that made my driver laugh. I laid my backpack aside and picked up the bottle from the floor. These two I thought are so full of themselves to verge on the side of carelessness.

I peered out of the window. It was almost dark, the heat of the day fading. Contemplating my next move I unscrewed the water bottle and took a large gulp. We were now on a country road having skirted what looked like a large town. A few miles on, now completely void of traffic with trees bordering both sides of the road ahead and a bend coming up, I decided to go for broke, and not an arm or a leg I hoped.

I went for it. Lunging forward I threw my manacled arms over the drivers head pulling back tightly on his throat. Instinctively he let go of the steering wheel attempting to free himself from my grasp, the car now out of control and amid the screams of his fellow officer we headed for an embankment that I was not aware of earlier. A final yell from the front seat and we were plunging down, the car rolling over once before landing on its side.

I stared down at my hands now miraculously free though still manacled, from where I had held the driver who now lay slumped over the steering wheel, then to the unconscious figure of the second officer, all the while music blared from the radio and the occasional click from the police channel.

I grabbed at the back of the front seat and succeeded in levering myself up. The driver lay motionless and I feared he might be dead. *Another charge against me. This time murder.*

Using my feet as battering rams I forced the door open and with a few positions I didn't know my body was capable of, threw myself out onto the grass. Winded, yet relieved to be alive I got shakily to my feet to take stock.

The car lay on its side almost at the foot of the slope, the second officer hanging half way out of the door. Although awkward with my hands in bracelets I succeeded in dragging him on to the grass and a snap examination told me that he probably had a head injury. I had no time to waste or feel guilty I had to make my escape before anything came along on the road above.

Should I search for the handcuff keys? A mobile phone? My first chance to phone Fenton? But even should I find a phone how did I explain where I was when I had no idea myself, and I sure as hell did not have the time to describe a country road and some sort of town we had passed through. On impulse I took the officers pistol from its holster, determined to use it rather than have Sowa take me prisoner. What the hell I thought, in for a penny in for a pound. In taking the pistol I saw the handcuff keys on his belt. I took them and while I made my way to the other side of the car intending to reach the road above, freed myself.

Although all things appeared to be against me, one thing was not, and that was my backpack hanging from a bush. Oh goody! I still have a clean shirt, and shook my head at the sure sign of going off my head? Was all this a nightmare and I'd wake up with a wee lassie staring at me over her seat in the plane? If only.

I reached the road and made sure that nothing was approaching either way, I started walking in the direction we were originally headed, deducing that as I was being taken to the prison not too far from Sowa's police station, the town that Mark lived in must also lie somewhere not too far away, considering the time I had been in the car.

Chapter 8

It was eerily dark now, and I was out of the tree line walking parallel to green pastures the vague outline of cows lying down for the night, I wishing that I could do the same.

Only one car had passed, forcing me to dive for a ditch, which thankfully I found dry. My one and only shirt would still be clean I thought sardonically.

Two hours later I was still walking, though somewhat slower. I had to rest. I climbed over or more precisely through a wire fence and into a field, seeking out in the half light the outline of a haystack. Thankfully I lay down in the side furthest from the road.

For a while I lay there. Though tired out by the days events I found sleep to elude me, my brain whirling with what to do next. For certain Sowa, receiving no response from the car radio would send another car or cars, to find out what had happened. I felt a chill and not from the night air, but the thought of the hanging man, or at least my fate in that notorious prison. I rose, it was no use, I couldn't sleep I might as well keep on walking.

However I did fall asleep behind a haystack in another corn field some two hours later.

It must be raining my face was wet. I opened my eyes, its tail wagging the little dog stood back. I blinked. "Thanks for the face wash," I yawned at the dog drawing a hand over where my little friend had licked me.

For answer it let out a few barks, and I held my finger to my lips. "That's enough, you'll wake up the place you wee mutt." Still my canine companion continued to bark. I looked darkly at it. "That's no language for a wee dog you should be ashamed."

Not quite sure what or who this two legs was, it cocked its head to the side.

I got stiffly to my feet and the dog stood back awaiting my next move.

I yawned and took a look around me. The field where I stood stretched a fair distance back to a small farmhouse, blue smoke rising lazily into the warm morning air. Opposite was the road on which I had walked from the car, to me a great distance on foot, but not so very far by car from where I had made my wee escape.

That was last night! Surely they had found the car and searched for me since then.

I tried to deduce what they would have anticipated my next move to be having survived the crash. I stared absently at the wee dog sitting there, it too wondering what I would do next.

One thing was sure I couldn't hang around here. This time to be caught was a life sentence, there were dead, or seriously injured men lying back in that car.

Tentatively I started down the road ready to jump into the ditch at the merest sound of a car. Should I leave the road, cross the fields and make my way from there? Happily my four legged pal had decided I was not fit company and had run off, back to its owner and breakfast I supposed. Lucky canine.

My decision not to leave the road almost proved fatal. It was the unmistakable sound of a truck approaching from behind that had me diving for a ditch, this time it was not dry. I lay cursing the ditch, the dog, the country, anything and everything I could think of as the dirty ditch water seeped through me.

The sound came from close above, and I dare not look up, instead fearing that I would be seen from the height of the truck I took a deep breath and ducked my head into the water. No apples here, I thought.

The sound faded then stopped all together. I lifted my head spitting out foul tasting water and took a cautious look, sliding quickly back into my ditch at the sight of the stationery truck less than a hundred yards away with grey clad soldiers clambering down from the back. Sowa had enlisted the army to find me!

I lay there staring up at a cloudless sky, wishing *beam me up Scotty* for there was no way that I could escape from here without being seen, as my only option was to run on the road back the way I had come or attempt to cross an open field, either was hopeless.

The soldiers drew closer. Anytime now and I would be discovered. Should I stand up now with my hands in the air, or take the chance of their stumbling across me and in their surprise let off a shot or two?

I heard a backfire, someone shouting, a wee dog barking, sounds of confusion. Whatever was going on I could not raise my head to find out.

I lay there soaking in the stench filled brown water, the sound of the truck slowly taking off followed by the sound of footsteps and a brown weather beaten face together with a wagging tailed wee dog staring down at me.

The weathered face said something, and I made a gesturing of not understanding and got up.

The old man laughed at me, and I laughed back. He was laughing at the state I was in, I laughing at not being caught.

He pointed to the tractor that obviously was the reason for the backfire, and I followed him to it, unslung my backpack and took a hasty look inside. There was no point in keeping the shaving soap, my once only clean shirt, dirty as I suspected as was my jacket. My novel too or what was left of it was slightly damp, and flicking through the pages debated whether to keep it or not, finally deciding that I wanted to know if the hero won through in the end or not, much like myself, I decided to keep it. We crossed the field my little pal sitting patiently beside me, now and again letting out a whimper, obviously at my smell.

At last we reached the farmhouse that I had seen earlier, my driver jumping down and calling out to someone inside.

That someone proved to be a woman about my driver's own age, no doubt his wife. I slid down and she gave me a look that said there's no work here, scarecrows are out of season.

Pointing at my jacket she gestured that I should take it off. I did so followed by my shirt, my trousers I decided to keep on though she did not think so.

After having washed under the outdoor cold water tap, the old lady waved me inside, no doubt having passed her inspection. She pointed that I should sit at the rough wooden table to what I could only describe as a plate of gruel. It was, my taste confirmed it. Anyhow I was grateful for food, even this set before me.

When I had finished, the old man vainly tried to ask me who and what I was, or so I construed by his hand gestures, and by his obvious frustration believed it would be better to ask my wee pal to translate for him.

The food had made me tired and the old woman pointed to a couch, laying her cheek on her hand to indicate that I should lie down.

I nodded my thanks and did as she suggested, my last thoughts as I drifted off were that I was safe here, it being obvious that my rescuer had no love for the army.

When I awoke I was at first mystified by where I was, it was midday or there about, the summer heat not quite having reached the coolness of where I lay. I sat up, the noise from the adjoining kitchen the only evidence that I was not alone. Yawning I rose and walked to the source of the sound. The old woman was busy at the stove, seeing me she smiled and nodded, pointing to a pot of coffee on the stove, I smiled and nodded back.

It was as I sat there that the shadow fell across the window and a girl in her late teens came in through the open door, and surprised by my unexpected presence drew to a halt.

My old hostess said something and the girl nodded.

"You are English?"she asked.

"Scottish actually," I replied.

"Ah" She turned to the woman said something then swung back to me. "My grandmother says the Federals are looking for you, we do not like the Federals. Why is this?"

"I think you mean why are the Federals hunting me?"

"Yes. Why is this so? Why do they look for a foreigner such as you? You must have done something really bad. I do not wish that my grandparents should be involved, you understand?"

Now at least I could converse with someone in my own language, in fact this little lady spoke better English than myself. Not difficult I grant you, however *I had learned how fur tae speak English as spoke in school*. My funny over and having a little time to think, I said, "A certain police officer wished to detain me until I could pay the sum he requested for my release." I saw her raise her eyebrows. "The charge was possession of drugs, of which I can assure you I am innocent. It is a little game he plays with anyone unfortunate enough to fall into his clutches should he believe them to be sufficiently rich to merit the effort. With me he made a mistake, I was neither rich nor the person he thought me to be."

I finished. Had my choice of words been too flowery in my attempt to have her understand me?

Seemingly the girl understood well enough to ask, "And who is this person you are not?"

I laughed at the description. "Let's just say that I cannot name names, only that they too do not like the Federals."

This seemed to satisfy her. "So where are you planning going from here? Grandmother says you escaped when the car that held you prisoner crashed, and that two men were injured."

Silently I was relieved to hear that neither my captors had died. "I was first taken prisoner with the intention of being taking to prison and held there until the money was paid for my release. Some people who also do not care for the police or the army freed me. I was taken to a house in a town I do not know the name of, from there they tried to help me to cross into Poland, however I was caught, but managed to escape." I spread my hands. "So here I am."

It was only a fraction of my exploits but I hoped it would satisfy my interrogator sufficiently to have me ask, "This town where I left from is somewhere in the direction from where I was first arrested, if I could get back I am sure those same people would help me again."

"You do not know any of their names? Without some clue as to who they are or the name of the town, I do not think it possible to help you."

"I can understand that. But is there no one whom you know that could help? My passport amongst other things were taken from me, including all my money."

"Perhaps." She thought for a moment. "I know someone who might be able to help." She thought again. "The problem is getting you into the town." She looked up at me from where she had studied the floor. "My name by the way is Kona."

"Pleased to meet you Kona, I'm West," I replied.

She returned to our problem with a nod. "I will speak to this man I think can help you. We must wait until market day."

My heart sank, readily expecting my helper to tell me it was a month from now, or their annual event which I had just narrowly missed. Instead she surprised me by saying. "We will go the day after tomorrow, this will also give me time to speak to this man that I know. Okay?"

"Okay," I grinned. What other choice had I?

The weather was stiflingly hot, even hotter that North Berwick on a good day. My eyes closed I sat soaking up the sun, my back against the farmhouse wall, thinking of my home town and wishing even if it was raining that I was back there right now, walking along the front admiring those brave enough to be wading or swimming, or just out for a walk, others playing on the putting greens. I sighed a deep sigh of home sickness. Oh to be home again.

At a sound of urgency I snapped my eyes open. The old farmer followed by his barking dog were running towards me, his arms flapping and pointing down the farm track where an army truck had drawn to a halt at the gate.

I jumped to my feet visions of my home forgotten, and my mind reeling with where to run to. The old farmer quickly gestured to follow him, which I did unhesitatingly, he led me to the barn further up the field.

I choked with fear and disappointment. The barn was the first place they would search, assuming it was me they were after and at this stage I thought it could be no one else.

The old man led me inside, his little dog barking unceasingly, a likely source I thought of giving me away. He pointed that I should follow him up the ladder to the loft and my heart sank even further at this being the most logical place for soldiers to look.

For a moment I hesitated, rapidly considering of taking my chances outside even should it entail running across an open field, better, I thought than being trapped in a hay loft.

The sound of the truck outside informed me I was too late, there was no option other than to follow the old man.

At the top, the old farmer ran across to the furthest corner, quickly, almost desperately throwing hay bales aside, I helped. Having now reached the bare wall he bent forward. I stared passed him fully expecting to see a small door of some sort, now the thumping of my heart had reached my feet at the thought that soldiers could not fail to see this, even if the farmer replaced the bales, worse still if he merely intended to cover me with hay.

To my surprise there was no door, instead with a grunt the farmer slid back a panel wide enough for me to crawl through, which I did without a moment's hesitation.

Once crouched inside, the small panel was slid back leaving me in the semi- darkness the only other occupant a wooden box filled by what looked like demijohns of wine. Obviously my rescuer had a side line going. And good luck to him I thought.

At first the only sound was the wee dog barking that told me the soldiers were in the barn. Then silence, and I hoped the farmer had taken his pet outside before some clever dick had the idea of carrying it up the ladder and have it sniff around, as a result of its incessant barking.

Putting my ear to the panel I listened for any sign of movement. At first I heard nothing until the panel gave a little shudder by my seekers moving the bales of hay. Involuntarily I moved back, my knees up to my chin in the small space, all the while expecting to see the panel move aside and the face of a soldier peering at me. Again the panel was hit by a bale, or a foot. So close yet so far I thought, followed a little later by receding voices. Then again silence.

I stretched out my legs as far as possible and let out a sigh. They were gone, or so I hoped. Now all I had to do was wait until the old farmer came to fetch me.

Then it came to me and I almost threw up at the thought. What if the soldiers found my jacket and backpack? Had they searched the house for me? Or had the soldiers decided that these kind folk knew nothing of my presence but that a stranger on the run might have taken the chance of hiding in their loft?

Somewhere in the distance I heard the dog barking excitedly, and the sound of soldiers laughter. They had not left, they were outside, and holding a party by the sound of it. I let my head rest against the wooden wall, resigned until they were on their way. At least I was free and had not been betrayed.

It was close on an hour I reckoned before I heard the noise in the loft outside, the panel drawn back and the toothless grin of the farmer beckoning me to come out. Clumsily I crawled through the tiny space almost falling as my legs gave way beneath me with cramp.

Chuckling, the old man grabbed me and had me sit on a bale until I had recovered. Then moving to the panel returned with a demijohn of wine, grinning and pointing to it as if this had all been a great joke.

A little later now partially recovered both physically and mentally from my recent ordeal I once again sat at the kitchen table. Kona put a plate of fried chicken in front of me and my appetite miraculously returned as had my jacket and backpack, which in my haste I had no time to look for, and which my rescuers had conveniently hidden.

"You like?" Kona pointed to the chicken.

"I like," I assured her grinning.

She sat down opposite me, lifted a leg of chicken from her own plate and began. "Tomorrow is market day in the town, grandfather will take you there to someone I think might help you. Okay?"

"Okay." I chewed my chicken scarcely able to wait for tomorrow.

Chapter 9

At long last tomorrow arrived, and for me none too soon.

By the kitchen clock quietly ticking away my life, I saw that it was not yet six. I gulped down what I assumed was porridge of some sort.

Kona stood over me when I had finished. "Grandfather will take you in his truck, I shall go by bicycle as usual. You will hide in the back, and remain there until I come to fetch you." She handed me an old pair of overalls. "Wear these, let us hope should you be seen that you are taken for one of us." Adding, "That old jacket you have been wearing will do."

Ignoring the comment about the jacket Mark had given me. I took the old garment, which had more holes in it than an MP's promise before election.

Kona looked amused. "Not Sunday wear." she apologised.

Nor any other day I thought, momentarily forgetting what risk these people were taking in helping me, and what could happen if caught.

When Kona had said that I would be hiding in the back of the old truck I hadn't thought to be sharing it with two rather large species of the pork chop variety, who snorting objections at my presence together with treading on my person, and on one or two occasions on a personal level while I attempted to bury myself under the tattered tarpaulin the old man had thrown over me, I lay there suffering and praying for the journey to end.

However all good things must come to an end including a hell of a journey to a market that seemed light years away. Eventually the truck drew to a halt. From where I lay I could just make out through a space between the cabin and mudguard, a busy cobbled square, filled with cattle and poultry but as yet no pigs, all held in some sort of pens. People shouting, others selling food and drinks, no doubt their version of McDonalds.

Now impatient I shoved a pig off my foot. How long must I lay here? Then a crunch of gears and we were on the move again, leaving the square to negotiate the descent of a narrow alley. Here at its foot in contrast to the market above, all was quiet as if what was taking place was in another town.

The old driver switched off the ignition; and I lay listening to the silence, all quiet except for the snorting of my fellow passengers. What now?

"Mr Englishman. Please to come."

It was Kona's voice that I heard. Cautiously I shook off the tarpaulin and raised my head above the side of the truck.

"Come, quickly." Kona beckoned me to follow her.

With a 'goodbye pals' to my four legged acquaintances I leaped over the side and ran after her where she had disappeared through a narrow doorway of a tall dark coloured building, ominous looking in comparison to that of the surrounding whitewashed houses.

Kona met me just inside the front door. "This way." She turned quickly, and I followed her up the stairs to the floor above, reaching there as she knocked on a heavy black wooden door.

When there was no answer, she looked at me and shrugged impatiently. "He said he would be here." She knocked again, this time the door opened, and the figure of a man beckoned us inside.

He was a stout wee man who begged us to be seated while he stood by the window.

His eyes quickly rested on me. "You are the foreigner who the Federals are seeking?"

"Yes, sir that's me."

A manservant placed a glass of wine in my hand, also offering one to Kona who refused with a slight wave of her hand.

"Kona tells me you were captured having been mistaken for some other person."

"That's correct. I was rescued and taken to some big house in a town I can neither name or describe I'm afraid."

"I see. Then twice you have attempted unsuccessfully to cross the border. Is this correct?"

"Yes." I sipped my wine while my host turned to stare apprehensively out of the window.

"And now I believe you should like me to try."

"If at all possible."

He turned back, "Kona also informs me you have neither money or passport."

Again I answered yes. "They were taken from me by a police officer by the name of Sowa. He originally took my own when he first retained me at his headquarters in a town I do not know the name of, but I understand was quite near a prison of some sort, where he intended to have me held until I, or my friends, could meet the amount of bale money required for my release."

The man who had not offered me his name, nodded. "Yes Kona told me something about this. A very nasty man. The type of man who when our revolution succeeds will receive his just deserts."

I took another sip of my wine admiring the man's command of English, also the first to enlighten me that he was part of this revolution he had mentioned, though I had no doubt that Mark and the others were part of the same anti government movement.

"This large house you mentioned, was it in the same part of the country as the prison this Sowa would have you imprisoned?"

"Yes. I should say by the time I spent in the car that took me there that it could be about a hundred kilometres or so. It was dark when we arrived, and as it stood a little distance from the main thoroughfare or so I believe, I have no way of knowing the name of the town."

The man nodded that he understood.

When Zofia or Andrias had left with me for the border I had in fact glimpsed a part of the town, but was reluctant to involve either by disclosing this to my host, on the off chance that this man might not be what he presented himself to be, and if so by naming names might well betray them to the authorities.

"You shall remain here until it is decided how best to get you back to Poland." My host said decisively.

He turned to Kona. "Please be careful. Go about your business as usual in the market. Now it is best that you say farewell to your friend, but be quick, your grandfather cannot deal with his pigs all by himself." He crossed to the door leaving us alone.

I quickly unbuttoned my borrowed overalls. "Your grandfather will want these back." I handed them to her. "Sorry about the smell, although the pigs didn't seem to mind," I said cheekily, thankful that I still had my jacket underneath.

Kona held out her hand, giving me an embarrassed smile. "I must not keep the pigs waiting, and like you I might not see them again."

"It's a while since I have been compared to pigs." I chuckled.

"Oh I did not mean to compare you with….."

Amused by her embarrassment I answered that I understood, then followed seriously. "Thank your grandparents for all their help and for also risking their lives for someone they did not know." I squeezed her hand. "And all you too have done. Maybe we will meet again, perhaps in my country where it is safer, or relatively so," I joked.

"Maybe Mr West Barns." She drew me to her and kissed me on the lips.

I choked back a little feeling of delight, my thoughts that if only she was a few years older. Reluctantly I released myself and holding her at arms' length I said dead pan, "You must go now, you cannot keep good pigs waiting."

"Yes, grandfather will be anxious for me." Then, clutching the old pair of overalls she was gone, out of the door and also my life.

I was flicking through my little novel in the room I had been given on the top floor of this large narrow built house when there was a knock at the door and what I took to be a manservant entered.

"Please," he began in broken English, handing me a white shirt, "this is for you."

Gratefully I took it thanking him. "Down stairs," he pointed at the floor, then mimed eating.

"Now?"

The wee man thought for a moment then taking my shoulder guided me to the door.

"Dinner must be on now," I said, "or maybe you only want me to peel the tatties (potatoes) is that it?"

There were seven men seated around the dining room table, two of whom were of my own age, the others forty to fifty years old. My host rose at my entrance. "Please to join us my friend," he greeted me pleasantly. "I know you are named West, my own name is George, these," he swept a hand over the room, "I will not name, you will understand."

"It would be pointless anyway, I can never remember names," I answered evenly, in turn nodding at faces smiling up at me, having obviously been accepted, probably at their bosses instructions, for this man could be nothing less.

George waved me to a seat. "You will take some of old Jacques wine, Mr Barns?"

By this I knew he meant the old farmer. "Yes, I surely will, I tasted some after the soldiers left yesterday."

Laughing he translated this to his guests who thinking the whole thing hilarious, raised their glasses to me, and I returned their salute, hoping there would be more such toasts to follow. After all it was an excellent little wine.

Later when the guests had left, George topped up my drink in the room he called his study.

"You will wear the shirt I left for you when we leave tomorrow, it is clean. The jacket you have will have to do, I do not have one to fit you."

Ignoring what he had said about the clothes I asked excitedly, "Where am I being taken this time?"

George sipped his drink, "To where there are people who may be able to help you. That is all you need know at present. My man will fill your backpack with bread and cheese and a few other niceties," he smiled "and some wine. We have a long way to travel."

I hesitated not knowing what response to my question would be. Finally plucking up courage I asked. "Is it at all possible that I might be allowed to contact my brother, let him know where I am, he must be worried, he has not heard from me since I left home. All he knows is what the newspapers are saying about me?"

I waited anxiously for the man's reply, though the answer when it came was no more than I had expected.

"I am afraid not, West. It is highly dangerous for all of us. Where we go tomorrow is very secret, and I am only taking you on the off chance there might be someone in another group with more opportunity to smuggle you across the border than I have. Do you understand my position? There might even be some who will question my decision to have me bring you along in the first place." George finished his wine putting his empty glass gently down on a small glass topped table. "Besides knowing that you are safe, what would be accomplished by your brother knowing you are here? Have him cross the border, and in so doing have himself arrested? You are after all wanted for drug possession; do you wish to make your brother an accomplice? He cannot help you back to Poland any more than we can, less I should say."

What the man was saying was true, yet it would have been good to have my big brother here even should it only be to assure me that everything would work out all right in the end.

Disappointed that I was to be denied hearing Fenton's cheery booming voice on the phone, I gave in graciously.

I should not have drunk so much wine, but I had longed for company, any company and the wine was a welcome substitute for this. Although I had seldom understood a word spoken at last night's little party, I had enjoyed the cheery atmosphere; at least I thought I had, however as I lay in bed my head spinning I had second thoughts, even some third and fourth ones. I lay there in this strange bed slowly descending as Mary Poppins, umbrella held high and clutching a protesting piglet under my arm, while folk such as Zofia Trudy and Kona held fingers to their noses, and the old farmer shouted up at me that he wanted back his overalls. Mercifully I fell asleep, just as Sowa fired, adding another hole to the old farmer's overalls.

It was George's manservant who awakened me. It was not quite dawn, and yawning I struggled out of bed. Beside me on a little table was a pot of steaming coffee, bread and cheese. Reluctantly I began to chew the bread not knowing whether it was this or the taste in my mouth that tasted foul, eventually I settled on my mouth.

I must have taken longer than my host intended me to take as the servant again appeared at my door beckoning anxiously for me to follow him. Sighing I picked up my bag and followed him downstairs.

In contrast to the warmth of the previous night, now the big room was cold dark and empty, George stood across the table sliding papers into a leather briefcase.

"Good morning, I hope you slept well?" His greeting was about as warm as the room, and I wondered whether he had had second thoughts about the wisdom of having me along.

"Yes thank you." I croaked.

"It is a long journey we have ahead of us." He pointed to a cloth bundle on the table, "Those are for the journey, it is the food I promised."

I mumbled a thank you and dropped the bundle into my bag on top of my newly acquired clean shirt.

George closed his briefcase with a click, and staring coldly across the table at me as though already having regretted agreeing to help me, said, "Now we are ready. Come."

It was a long journey, and an even longer day. Though I had slept for most of it I still felt the effects of the previous night, craving water rather than food, although I had demolished my bundle together with the 'niceties' in my backpack.

I screwed up my eyes and took a brave look out of the side window of the back seat of the large black car in which two other men travelled. They had not spoken or attempted to speak to me the entire journey, which gave me a good reason for ignoring them and closing my eyes.

From the front seat, George swung round and indicated ahead. Nodding I followed where he pointed.

There, a little way ahead perched precariously on the rocky hillside was the outline of a town, the spire of a church dominant to the cluster of whitewash walled houses surrounding it. We entered through what in bygone days no doubt had been a portcullis into a large cobbled square, and I was pleasantly surprised by the small bistros and shops lining each side of the square, each lit up outside by various coloured lights, all of it appeared to my astonished eyes not short of clients enjoying themselves sitting at the outside tables.

However our driver did not halt but seemingly knowing where he was going left the merriment of the square, rounding a corner to stop at the entrance of a moderately looking hotel.

One of my non conversant travelling companions was the first to get out of the car where he proceeded to open the boot and hand out our luggage, including mine which he scowled at contemptuously.

"Don't blame me pal," I glared at him, "This is not the place I booked my holiday. I must have a word with my travel agent when I get back, *If I get back I added under my breath.*"

George led the way and we followed. It was evident that we were all expected, as all I had to do was take a room key and make my way to the third floor, together with instructions from my benefactor to make short work of a shower and meet him and the others in the main dining room. This I did but only after quietly debating whether or not to forego the shower and shave, for a quick nap on top of the inviting looking comfortable bed. My stomach won and I left for the dining room.

It was not difficult to find should the sound of laughter have anything to go by. My feeling when entering the room I could only describe as 'strangely strange' never having felt so out of place before. Perhaps it was the strange tongue that made me this way, or that I was a stranger completely at the mercy of other strangers for their help. However my 'strangeness' was not to last long, for rising from a table where she had been dining with a few others, Zofia hurried to greet me.

"So you have survived West Barns!" her eyes gleaming with what I could only describe as genuine delight Zofia pulled me to her kissing me on the cheek.

Aware that everyone was watching, or almost everyone, I could only make some sort of face signifying that this was so, but at the same time felt a right 'eejit'

"And so have you." I beamed at her, my embarrassment momentarily forgotten. "How did you do it? Where did you go?"

Zofia did not answer my questions but instead led me by the hand back to her table, where Andrias and Serge rose, both apparently happy to see me again.

"We only heard yesterday that you were alive, West," Serge shook my hand eagerly.

"Lucky for you that you met George" Andrias clasped my hand from across the table.

I sat down, someone pushing what seemed a whole plate of chicken in front of me, another adding potatoes to it.

"You must eat before it is all gone. You are late arriving." Andrias urged me. "And should you wish dumpling you must eat even faster, before Serge here devours the lot!" he laughed, with the others joining in.

I had no opportunity to ask Zofia how she had made her escape as the others at our table were hell bent on enjoying the evening, Serge a little put out by my reluctance to imbibe as freely as my friends, I having remembered my last 'imbibe 'of not so long ago.

The meal over, Andrias leaned close to my ear shouting to be heard above the rising volume of merrymakers, asking how I had escaped, only to be interrupted by someone calling out my name. I looked up at Mark standing there, once again having my hand shaken vigorously, while he said, "So we meet again West Barns, obviously you have not made it home."

"No," I grinned at him, "I am your preverbal boomerang."

He shook his head in understanding. "We must speak later. But please for now I have other matters to discuss," he added apologetically.

A little later I lost Zofia to Serge, and left to my own devices sat down in a corner of the room watching with amusement this gathering of men and women in various degrees of intoxication, thinking smugly, that this time I should be free of what they were about to feel like in the morning. However I was not sufficiently inconspicuous that the burly figure of Arnau still sought me out, coming at me, hand already outstretched in greeting.

"You did not make it my friend, eh!" he beamed at me.

"I see that you are overcome by sadness that I did not," I answered dead pan.

He slapped me on the shoulder. "You know what I mean. I such as anyone wish you safely home."

"Thanks."

"You have no drink? What, you are sad to be here?"he asked seriously.

"I really don't know what this all about, only that I am told that there might be someone here who can help me reach Poland."

Arnau flipped his hand, "Maybe yes, maybe not. I will ask at our conference tomorrow. Okay?"

Now was the time I thought to ask about Trudy. "Trudy is not here, or the doctor? They are both well, I hope."

Arnau shook his head. "No, they cannot be spared, besides it is mainly the group leaders who are here to represent their own people. As to your second question, yes they are both well. I shall tell them you ask for them when I return." Then he too, excusing himself, left, no doubt to seek out more congenial company than myself.

I sat back and carefully sipped a little of my wine. Although I had guessed it Arnau had more or else confirmed my suspicion that this was a high level Groups' conference, and my presence here was probably either indeed an attempt to help me home, or just to keep a careful eye on me until they decided my fate, and here was the ideal place to do so. This time I took a larger swallow of my drink, having suddenly felt uneasy at the thought.

It was close on midnight before I saw Zofia again, she picked me out sitting in the corner by myself.

"West, you are alone. Do you not care for our company?" she made a mou pretending to be sad.

"Oh, I enjoyed everyone else enjoying themselves, it makes a change from being hunted."

She sat down across from me and leaned a little unsteadily on the table.

"What happened West? I only caught a glimpse of you running to the gate of the station, then I saw you stopped by the police."

"Yes it was Sowa. He had me held in some police station or other."

Zofia' s face lost most of its colour, fear in her eyes. "You were held by Sowa?"

"Yes he wanted to know where I'd been since you lot first freed me. Understandable of course," I chuckled. In no way did I intend speaking of my situation or the tortured man.

Zofia's eyes followed the last of the night's revellers leaving, and once again I saw fear in her eyes. "West you must not tell anyone that you were arrested, especially not by Sowa, even should he only be police and not Federal," she pleaded, searching my face for assurance.

"Were certain people to know..."

"Don't worry," I reassured her, "I didn't give anything away. How could I? I did not even know the name of the town and still don't where Mark lives. I told them I was blindfolded most of the time. I only told them what they already knew, how the Federals raided the farm house after my release, followed by the long drive the very long drive to the town I didn't again know. I know that was a lie, but I hoped to give the impression that I had been taken to the other side of the country."

By her look I knew I had did little to convince her that I had not given any information away that might lead Sowa or the Federals to any of the Groups, especially to the one in the mountains. Now I understood her fear for me. I knew too much about Mark, Arnau and now George including herself Serge and Andrias.

"Honest Zofia, as I said, I only told them what they already knew."

"And George? How did you come to know him?"

This I confess was another problem. "It was the farmer's granddaughter who sheltered me after I crashed the police car on my way to prison, and my consequence escape that she had me meet George, and he decided to bring me here with the purpose of finding someone to help me reach Poland."

Zofia held her head in her hands. "This gets worse, West. Who else knows about your dealings with our groups, maybe the odd peasant on your way to buy a paper, or something?"

The last thing on my mind was to find myself angry at a girl who had put her life on the line to save me.

I stood up, "That's all I can say, Zofia. I told them nothing, nothing at all that could connect any of you with me. All they know from me is that it was a female who helped me to the station, and one man in the car who was shot on that first attempt. Is this good enough for you?"

Zofia too rose. "I suppose it will have to do, but as I said, say nothing more about your escape."

"Which one?" I added sarcastically. Then, "Goodnight, Zofia, sleep well."

Chapter 10

I breakfasted late that next morning, with the intention of missing my companions, or their companions, or perhaps the word should have been 'comrades' all of this I was not sure.

My breakfast over I took a casual aimless stroll across the square, it was early and the empty bistros were preparing for another busy day. I looked at a few shops, only one or two I noticed catered for tourists, but unlike myself ones with money.

Eventually, my feet led me to the wall encircling most of the town, brown Marina sheep in the meadow below. A little distance away a shepherd boy of around fourteen with a barking dog at his heels drew closer, he waved, shouting something I did not understand, probably something like "I don't suppose ye have a fag on ye by the way" in a broad Glaswegian accent, well you never know we Scots get everywhere. I returned the wave feeling much better at having found a friend, even though a distant one.

The day dragged on, and I mulled over what my fate which was most probably the topic of discussion at the group conference right now would be. Should I just up and leave? Try for Poland on my own? Stupid of course without transport, passport or money. Besides, I laughed which way *was* Poland? Out the gate and turn left? Sad, I turned back to my hotel. At least there I did not have to pay for my coffee.

The evening meal passed pleasantly enough, for me that was, though none of my so called friends made reference as to my future, or should that be 'fate'. Meal over, Zofia made a little sign that she wished to talk. Silently we both strode to the door, where outside she turned to face me. "Let's walk for a little, West."

Still silent I walked beside her. She pointed to a bistro across the square. "We shall have a coffee." Her voice though soft held a note of resignation, and I wondered if she had been left to break the news to me that I was to be shot at dawn, or at most a few minutes after.

"Only if you're paying?" I said as cheerily as I could manage.

"What?" My question puzzled her.

"Only if you are paying for the coffee, I'm skint." I corrected myself, "Sowa the greedy bas...., stole all my money for a second time," I added, "or more precisely, Mark's money."

My explanation appeared to annoy her. We sat down, and when served, Zofia drew her coffee to her. "They all know about your being captured by Sowa. Some feel that you could not have failed to disclose what you know of us." She looked at me the obvious question in her eyes asking what *had* I told the fat captain.

I let out a long deep sigh, suddenly tired of all this, this endless nightmare. "I have already explained that Sowa knows nothing about your group activities from me." I made a cutting motion with my hand. "End of story. Either you believe me or you don't. And right now strictly speaking I could not care less."

Zofia sipped her coffee and gently put her cup into the saucer. Still looking at it and not me, she said softly, "It was thought best that you return with Arnau until we try again to get you to Poland."

I focused on the top of her head as she sat staring into her cup, well aware of my reaction. For me to return to that mountain 'retreat' was not the word I was looking for, was out of the question. "No way," I shot at her angrily.

At last she raised her head to look at me. "I thought this would be your answer. But West you must consider it." She sounded desperate, "there is no alternative."

"For who? Them or me?" I asked bitterly.

Her silence gave me the answer. Now I really was in danger.

"You think my knowing of your various groups endanger you all?" I swept a hand around me. "What about these people here in this place, are they all completely reliable? Are they all anti-government? Quite a bob or two to be made having you all together in one basket so to speak by someone informing the Federals, or the police for that matter. A much bigger risk than me I should think."

Dismissing my theory Zofia shook her head. "Anyone informing on us would be swiftly dealt with."

"Not if all of you are caught, or even worse, dead."

"I don't mean by us, West, by their fellow villagers. That is why we are safe here. Besides these people are our friends and look forward to our coming."

And who else I thought, thinking back to my own failed attempts, never having shrugged off the feeling of having been betrayed.

"Excuse me, but are you the foreigner?" The man who had interrupted our conversation was a small weedy man, someone I expected to find flogging watches or some other articles of dubiety on a street corner.

"I am," I answered sitting back in my chair the better to inspect this intruder in the shabby grey suit, quite glad of the interruption.

"May I sit?" the wee man indicated a chair opposite me. My nod had him continue as he sat, "It is your intention to reach Poland, I believe." My stare was enough to have him go on. "In this I may be of assistance... for a price."

A price there was always a price. "Go on I'm listening."

"I could have you across the border in three days time for as little as two thousand Euros paid in advance of course."

"Naturally," I said sarcastically. "Except I don't have two thousand Euros, at least not here. However should you trust me, I can have that amount sent to you once I'm over the border. My brother would see to it straight away."

The wee man shook his head. "Sadly I must have the money in advance, expenses you understand."

"How can you do this, when we have failed?" Zofia asked our guest suspiciously.

"Your attempts were by road, I presume, not by plane?"

"Airports are a far greater risk, there are photographs of the wanted at every checkout. Once in the building there is no escape."

Zofia's voice had been scathing, and I fully expected the man to jump up and leave, instead he returned her sarcasm with a twist of his lip. "Who said anything about an airport? This is why I require such a large sum of money. Fuel alone will be expensive, and there is the pilot to bribe, amongst other things."

Suddenly my hopes rose. Leaving from a deserted field somewhere, could succeed. The man saw that he had convinced me. "I will have to think about it. If you won't take my word about the money I will have to raise it elsewhere. Can you give me until tomorrow?"

The wee man rose. "It must be early, your friends leave tomorrow." He took a step away, turned and said. "Meet me over by the wall at seven. Okay."

When my so called rescuer had left, Zofia's eyes met mine, "You will trust him about what he said about the plane? It is most likely you will mysteriously disappear on the way there, perhaps in the exact field he has persuaded you he will use for your getaway."

"So what difference should that make to you? If not your lot, why not him? After all you said yourself everyone here could be trusted."

Zofia looked astonished. "We are not murderers, Mister West Barns, whatever else you may think of us."

I was determined not to be taken in by such indignation, righteous or otherwise. "Okay if not, then the feasible thing to do is have Mark or some other rich member of your organisation loan me the money."

The way Zofia rose, I knew I had angered her. "Then you must ask Mark or someone else you think has such funds." She turned with a not very warm, "Goodnight West, no doubt I will see you in the morning."

I sat for a moment, the square was emptying, except for one bistro that appeared to enjoying a few late night customers, two of which were Serge, an old man I had not seen before and the young shepherd boy, all three sat laughing, obviously enjoying the evening. Eventually the old man and the boy said their good-nights to Serge who remained sitting quietly finishing his drink.

I watched Serge for a few minutes, mulling over asking his advice about trusting my wee man before deciding that he was not likely to help me having already tried and failed.

Eventually I rose and returning to my hotel, and finding out Mark's room number decided to pay him a visit.

Mark opened the door, already dressed for bed. "Sorry to disturb you Mark, can I have a word?"

"If it is important." He stood aside to let me in, a look of annoyance on his face, leaving me to stand there while he took a seat. "Well how can I help you?" he crossed his legs under his silk bed robe exchanging his look of annoyance to one of anger.

I told him about my encounter with the wee man and his offer of help together with his price.

"You know this man's name?" Mark asked reaching for a cigarette from a box on a table beside him.

"No. Although I thought you might. Zofia was there during the discussion but she too did not appear to know who he was."

"A villager, most likely," Mark lit his cigarette. "So is it your intention to take up this offer of his?"

I leaned against a wall desk and looked down at him. "That all depends on you. Should you see your way to lend me the money, I'd have it returned to you pronto, my brother Fenton would see to that until I had my own stolen credit card replaced. You know the one Sowa took from me that first day." *A million years past I thought.*

"Ah that brings us nicely to Sowa." Mark sat back casually in his chair and watched the smoke from his cigarette drift towards the ceiling. "He had you detained for quite some time did he not?"

"No he did not, although it did seem so at the time."

"But long enough for him to find out all about us? Correct."

I levered myself off the desk, and sprang towards him. Frightened by what I might do, Mark leapt to his feet, my words reaching him across the room in one loud blast. "I'm sick of this, you, Zofia and all the rest. For the last time Sowa learned nothing from me as to who or what you are. And what I did tell him he already knew. Now I should think if you do not believe me it would be in your interest to lend me the money and let me get the hell out of here, out of your hair and this god forsaken country!"

Shaken and fighting to regain his composure Mark sank slowly into his chair. "We honestly tried to help you reach Poland, West, we really did. It was our mistake in the first place that you were mistaken for someone else and we owed it to you to try. Sowa in his greed and determination to keep his little scheme secret tried to have you hid away so that he could blackmail you and your friends into paying for your release. Having retained your passport it made it decidedly more difficult for us." Mark waved a hand, "as you already know of course."

Mark drew nervously on his cigarette. "I will not help you with the money, West. Not because I do not want to, but I don't believe this man's plan will work. And should it fail and you and your so called rescuer are caught, you might find it difficult not to give Sowa should it be him, or others equally expert at extraction information, what they want to know."

My anger disguised my disappointment. "So where do I go from here?" I threw myself in a chair across from my one time benefactor.

"Probably what Zofia has already suggested that you do, return with Arnau to the mountains until we can try again to get you home. In the meantime I will seek out this man you speak of and ask him a few questions as regards the practicality of his plan."

Beaten I rose, Mark now completely back to his old confident self, though wary of a Scotsman with a hidden but violent temper, though I wondered how much damage that same temper might have cost me.

It is understandable that I did not sleep well that night, and my first action was to jam a chair against my door before slipping the policeman's pistol under my pillow, fortunately no one called to pay me a visit.

Next morning I ate breakfast by myself. No one I knew attempted to speak to me, although Arnau gave me a few curious looks from where he sat at his table.

Eventually I rose and walked to the town wall where I had agreed to meet my wee rescuer, at least there was nothing to lose by meeting him again in the hope he might reconsider awaiting payment after I reached Poland. Dream on I told myself. However he was not there, and it was now 7 am.

Now what to do was my next thought. Would I indeed have to leave with Arnau after all? The feeling made me feel sick. Should I in fact have no other alternative, would I be left to rot away there? Or perhaps they planned a swifter end for me. My only consolation was that I might see Trudy again, though not even that changed my perception of the place.

I hitched my backpack on to my back, at least I was ready to leave for all I possessed was in it.

I leaned on the wall contemplating my next move, at first unaware of the same shepherd boy as yesterday, running towards the village waving his arms wildly and pointing agitatedly towards the road beneath him

Not taking too much notice I casually followed the pointing finger. There on the brown winding road below, a column of army trucks sped towards the village. Federals! I choked.

I ran shouting my warning to everyone within range. At the end of the square some of the other groups were busy loading their cars, ready to be on their journey home. "Soldiers!" I shouted pointing to the entrance. "Soldiers! Federals!"

The last word seemed to jerk them into action. One man ran into his hotel another to alert others. I ran round the corner to my own hotel, where Mark was in the act of closing the boot of his car.

"Mark!" I shouted, "There are truck loads of soldiers on their way here!"

Wordlessly Mark ran into his hotel colliding with Zofia coming out, shouting my warning to her.

Shooting a glance at me she dropped her luggage and took off down the alleyway. I didn't know what to do, whether to follow her or make myself scarce. No way did I want to be involved in what I knew was about to happen.

I shot back to the square where two cars sped towards the entrance, my thoughts that there was no way past the oncoming trucks on that narrow road. My thinking was wrong, for once there the cars screeched to a halt blocking the entire entrance.

Suddenly there were armed men arriving from every direction into the square. A hand appeared on top of the wall followed by the sweating face of my young shepherd boy. I grabbed him by both shoulders and helped haul him over.

Muttering his thanks he ran off across the square towards one of the bistros as the first of the mortars landed with a clump, throwing tables and chairs skywards followed by another hitting a parked car, screams of terror erupting from those inside. Another mortar landed on the cobbles, shards of stone flying in all directions.

This was no place for me I decided, these soldiers meant to annihilate the village, for what I had seen of their strength by the number of trucks, they could just as easily have surrounded the village without bloodshed.

Mark together with Serge and Arnau ran past me, the three armed to the teeth, plainly prepared for such an emergency as I had not seen any weapons in the car boot that had brought me here.

Now I was on my own, but where to run or hide? The soldiers would not distinguish me from anyone else here, especially dressed as one of them.

The houses and bistros on either side of the square were now ablaze, firing had broken out close to the entrance. I took a hasty look over the wall where a long line of grey clad soldiers crossed the meadow on their way here.

Another explosion, another car thrown in the air. "Better get yersel' oot o' here, West!" I shouted aloud and began to run, or in my case at a speedy hobble owing to my gammy leg back down the alleyway past my hotel. Grey soldiers appeared from nowhere, confirming they were already over the wall. I melted into a doorway thinking should I defend myself, use my pistol or merely stand with my hands in the air and shout out in English who I was, or just hope for the best?

The soldiers were too close now for me to unhitch my backpack for my weapon. A shout arose followed by the rapid fire of a submachine gun, a soldier fell at my feet then another.

Silence then a moan. Terrified I stood there wishing the locked door behind me would fly open and I could disappear inside. I ventured a look, and stared down into the tortured face of Arnau lying there, a pool of blood widening from where he'd been hit in the gut.

"Tell Trudy..."

That was as far as the fatally wounded man got, and for the first time I would have given anything to be on my way with him to the mountains.

I continued to run down the same narrow alley that Zofia had earlier, perhaps she knew of an escape route, or was she just blindly running away from the sound of firing? I ran, almost reaching a corner, Andrias came running towards me, pointing his submachine gun and calling out something that I could not make out, then he was down, writhing on the cobblestones. I swivelled round but whoever had shot Andrias was nowhere to be seen. But why had he wanted to shoot me? Or was he aiming past me at someone behind?

No time to ponder, I kept on running.

I had almost reached the foot of the alley where the body of a woman lay. Cursing the whole world and beyond, I heard a moan and an arm raised weakly for help. I drew to a halt, panic stricken at the thought of being caught here in the open. The hand beckoned and I took a hasty step forward, horror stricken, for the figure was that of Zofia. I knelt down my fear temporarily forgotten.

"West," It was little more than a whisper. "Serge."

"I will tell him," I promised, though how I did not know.

She gasped, her face twitched with pain, and I dared not look where she had been hit.

"Your book 75". Then the eyes glazed over and she was gone.

The sudden sound of gunfire from the top of the alley had me again on my feet and running.

I heard a shout, it was the young shepherd boy waving to me, he stood there with the shotgun over his shoulder, his open sleeveless sheepskin jacket revealing a tanned body, a colourful bandana round his head. Again he waved desperately to me.

I ran to where he stood by the wall. He said something quickly in his own tongue, then realising I did not understand stared at me as though I had just arrived from outer space and I wished I had and Scotty could beam me up. "I only speak English," I said hurriedly.

"Ah! Down, we must climb down there."

I took a quick look. The wall was built on top of sheer rock, some thirty feet or so high.

The boy saw my look of hopelessness. "Wait here." Then he was off and running.

I thought wait? Where else can I run to? All the while the sound of gunfire grew louder.

A few more *long* minutes passed and the boy was back carrying a length of rope.

"There! Over there!" He pointed to a large hand cart full of vegetables standing in a corner. He took off and I followed, already wise as to what he intended.

Pushing, swearing panting we manoeuvred the cart to the wall. A sudden burst of gunfire now much closer than the last had us spin round, both fully expecting to see grey uniforms heading in our direction, saying nothing we let out a sigh of relief the boy tying the rope to a wheel of the cart and throwing the other end over the wall.

I stepped to the wall and peered down, the boy by my side. "It's a bit short, as all the lassies have told me," I said seriously.

"What?"

"Never mind, kid only a bad joke."

The boy jumped up on top of the wall. "I will go first."

I looked up at him grasping the rope in both hands. "Be careful, kid it's still a fair drop."

He nodded and I held my breath watching him slide down the rope, until reaching the end, with the confidence of youth let go and dropped easily to the ground.

Giving up a silent prayer with the hope that the Big Man was at home, I threw down my young friends shotgun to him and cautious or to be more precise terrified, grasped the rope and began a shocking version of an abseiling monkey, my hands nipping with the strain of holding on. Almost at the bottom I looked down to where the boy held what was left of the rope as rigidly as possible. No more rope, I let go and shifted my balance so that my 'good' leg would take the fall. It worked, well partially, for I landed in a heap and the boy helped me to my feet.

Still a bit dazed and hurting a little, the boy grabbed me by a shoulder, "fast!" he shouted in my ear, lifting his gun, and I ran behind him to a cluster of bushes nearby.

Above us, already on the rope a soldier had started his descent.

"Come on! let's go!"I shouted ready to run with intention of keeping the bushes between us and the soldiers above. Instead the boy raised his shotgun and as the soldier was about to jump from the end of the rope, fired and hit, the soldier fell to the ground.

I let out an oath I had once heard in the Glasgow Gorbals. "Come on, the rest will come down after us!" And I was away before I had finished my warning, the boy hotly following.

We were well on our way before I had the courage to halt and look back, and much to my relief there were no soldiers following, only one or two clustered around their stricken mate.

My companion gave me a look. "I did wrong?"

"You sure did wee man. We're lucky they have bigger fish to fry than us."

"Why should they wish to fry fish, mister?"

Amused, I shook my head. "It's only a saying, it means they have more on their plate than us."

"But we are not on a plate," he said with a puzzled expression.

"Forget it son, it's just an old Scottish expression."

We were now running and hiding parallel to the stationary trucks lined up on the road. Firing still reached us from the village.

"Where will you go now, son? You can't return to your village just yet."

He nodded, his face solemn. "Please, I go with you."

"I don't think that's a good idea, I'm headed for Poland."

He made a face. "That is a long way. How do you try to get there?"

"I have to try," I used his expression. "to get there, before your soldiers or police catch me."

The boy's face lit up. "Then I will help you." He spat on the ground. "That is what I think of them."

I did not ponder the offer. Perhaps this boy could help me, considering there was no one else.

"Okay, but if you do you had better start by telling me your name."

"It is Jan."

"West." I held out my hand.

"So happy to meet you mister West."

"Same here, Jan."

I looked around me. Which way?"

Jan pointed to the mountains beyond the trucks. "That way, but the way is long."

"Shorter if we can steal a truck."

Jan's face lit up. "But how?"

I pointed to the last vehicle. "There's no one in that jeep, those soldiers standing around are a good hundred yards up the road. Come on, let's give it a try."

We set off dodging in and out of protesting sheep, and I noted that all sheep 'ba' in the same language, reaching the foot of the embankment at the side of the narrow road.

I lifted my head and took a cautious look. "It's a left hand drive, the wheel is on the other side."

Jan's stare clearly said that everyone knew that, so what was my problem?

"Sorry," I apologised, "I'm going to make a dash for the driver's side. Wait here until I know whether there are any keys in the ignition, if so I will start up, you be ready to jump aboard. When you do, keep a sharp lookout for those soldiers up the road, I'll not be able to see them because of the truck in front. Okay? Do you understand me, Jan?"

The boy nodded that he did and I slowly clawed myself up the grass banking. *One* glance up the road, *one* deep breath and I was across the road and in between the jeep and the narrow mountainside, my eyes searching the steering wheel and hopefully the keys. I was in luck they were there.

I quickly divested myself of my backpack, threw it into the back and clambered into the driver's seat, turned on the engine, and shouted to Jan to climb aboard.

I switched on the ignition cursing at first not knowing where the throttle was then the floor pedal, revved up and shifted into reverse, Jan leaning out of the side his eyes on the soldiers so very little distance away, ready to tell me if they had heard the jeep start up or not.

The road was narrow with little room to turn around.

"They have heard you mister West!" Jan, sounded frantic, which was no wonder considering what these same soldiers had done to his village. "They are running! We will not make it!" Shots zipped past enforcing Jan's alarm. "My gun! I have left it in the grass!"

I accelerated back, felt the tail hit the mountainside, and turned the wheel full lock, and with inches to spare faced down hill. Then we were off.

The shotgun obviously forgotten in the excitement Jan shouted, "We made it West! We made it!"

My foot to the floor, I shouted, "what do you mean *we*!"

Offended Jan shot me a look.

Relieved by what we had done together and to eradicate my mistake at my misplaced humour, I gave his shoulder a gentle punch. "Only kidding wee man, only kidding you did well."

Whether or not he understood me, or like myself only too happy to be on our way he threw his head back laughing. "Okay mister West. OK."

A continual look behind informed us no one was following, it was taking time for jeeps further up the column to extricate themselves from amongst the trucks.

"Where do we go from here, wee man?" I asked my navigator.

"There is a small road on the right a few kilometres from here, it will take us through the hills to the mountains we must climb to reach your Poland."

I glanced at the boy in dismay. "You never said anything about climbing mountains!"

Jan chuckled. "You never asked me. Not to worry West I know a way through the passes. My grandfather took me when I was little. He did much business in Poland." He shot me a wicked look.

"OK as long as I don't have to climb anything higher than North Berwick Law."

"What law is this West? Why should a mountain have a law?"

"Never mind kid, it would all be uphill me trying to explain it to you, just let me say it is the name of a hill back home."

Chapter 11

I judged it to be close on an hour before Jan who had been half asleep pointed ahead.

"There is the road, West. We go up there."

Doing as I was asked I turned on to a steep and narrow brown road, a little apprehensive that the dust the jeep was throwing up could be seen by anyone following.

Jan seemed to understand my concern. He took a look back. "No one is coming, West."

"Good, but if and when they do they are sure to see our tyre marks." Changing gear I asked, "Where does this road lead?"

"Many kilometres. We will pass through a little…place," he struggled for the correct word, "my grandfather Petrovic lives in a hut, cabin, on the hill."

"I thought your grandfather lived with you back in the village?"

He nodded. "That is mother's father. This one here belongs to my father."

The jeep hit a rut and I had to change gear. "I see. Where are your parents, Jan, if you don't mind me asking?"

"Both are dead." He sighed. "It is a long story."

And although his telling me would help pass the time, somehow I thought it best not to ask.

Later I stopped at a spot that gave me an unobstructive view of the road.

I stretched myself. "How far now, Jan?"

"Many kilometres."

I stepped to the jeep. "See if there is any food in the back, Jan, I'm feeling a bit peckish." I asked, my eye on the fuel gauge which I was pleased to see still registered half full.

"There is this, West." Jan held up a canvas sack.

"Take a look inside." I turned while he undid the leather straps.

"This." Jan held out a satchel. "It's says it is soup."

"Good,"I sighed, "cold soup. Anything else?"

Jan's face lit up, "Only this, it is some kind of chocolate." He threw it to me.

I had to take the boy's word for it as I could not understand the label. "Okay." I broke off a piece and threw it to him, which he bit into eagerly and with his eyes gleaming, said in delight, "It is good, West, it is good!"

Tentatively I took a bite, and made a face. "Don't agree with your taste, Jan." I said in disgust.

I pretended to look around. "I don't suppose there is a McDonald's anywhere near?"

"No but there is one in Krakow, I have seen it."

"There's nothing I rather be doing now, than being there with you, even should it only be for a coffee." There was no pointing in wishing. I had to do something about it. McDonald's or Krakow were not about to come to me.

We started again, Jan handed me one of the three metal water bottles he'd found, gratefully I took a swallow and handed it back.

"Is there any stream, or river in this barren looking land," I asked, "What water we have will not last long in this heat?"

"No, West, nothing until we reach the village of Grandfather Petrovic."

I was about to ask how far away was that was when it happened, swinging round a corner on the narrow road I had hit the rock before I knew it, coming to an abrupt and unceremonious halt.

Cursing I jumped down to inspect the damage.

"It is the rocks that have fallen from up there," Jan pointed up the hillside.

"A landslide," I growled, "in this weather?"

"Storms cause it West, they happen very quickly."

"Out of the blue," I did not laugh at my own pun.

I stared around at the empty brown landscape, surrounded by fair sized hills.

"Where to now, Jan? Any ideas? I took a step towards the tons of rock blocking our way, that we had not a hope in hell of moving."

Jan pointed to the oil gushing from beneath the jeep. "The jeep it will not go, it is as you say f...."

I stopped him from completing the adjective. "Okay, I get it."

"Then we must walk."

"I know, but where?" I looked around me. "I don't even see a goat track, and don't say we're the goats, or you'll get a punch of fives."

Jan shook his head in laughter.

I took another far from hopeful look beneath our former transport, shook my head and stood back.

"The road goes in and out of those hills," Jan pointed in the direction we were taking before our unexpected halt. He turned to point at the hills above us. "the village is not so far away, if we go that way."

"How far, is not so far, Jan?" I wanted to know, but yet I didn't.

"Two days, maybe less."

"*Two days!*" I exclaimed totally unprepared for such an answer. "We only have a cupful of water or so, and if you expect me to eat that... that... sh.... you gave me, I might as well save myself the trouble and wait for the army to catch us, or me up." I amended.

"If I was to tell you there is a McDonald's in the village would that help?" Jan asked, his eyes squarely on mine awaiting my reaction.

"And Scotland might win the world cup," I replied sarcastically.

"Okay no McDonald's, no world cup. So what do you do now. Myself I will go up there and will return from my village with some food."

"From McDonald's I suppose," I grinned, understanding the boy's ploy. "Okay" I said in resignation, and leaned over to see what else was in the back of the jeep.

The sun was at its Zenith when we finally halted for a well earned rest in the shade of a few high boulders.

"It will rain soon," Jan confirmed, staring up at the deep blue sky.

"No chance." I yawned, "there's not a cloud in the sky."

"They come." The boy rose. "I think we go and look for a place before it rains very heavily."

I could have lain there stretched out all day, but I had the feeling my young fellow traveller knew what he was talking about. Stifling another yawn I got wearily to my feet.

Jan pointed "Your shoes will not last."

"Neither will my feet if you keep up this pace, I'm not quite in the mountaineering league you know."

"Mountain people have a league? They play football?"

I threw Jan a look asking if he was pulling my leg, and if so which one, my gammy one was already throbbing in time to my swear words.

However he had walked away before I had the chance to ask him.

Jan was correct in his assumption that it would rain, what he had failed to inform me to expect, was just how heavy, until I believed it must be the Glasgow Fair holidays.

We ran, Jan guiding me to the side of a hill where at this distance there appeared to be a small cave of some sort. Some sort was right, when closer my cave turned out to be nothing larger than a niche in the rocks.

"We can shelter here." Jan declared appearing to be satisfied with our shelter.

"How do we do that, take turns at standing outside? Or on one another's toes?" I had not intended to sound so miserable, but I was.

Jan's answer was to back into our hole and sit down. He opened my backpack that he'd carried for me since leaving the jeep, holding up the so called tablet that I so hated. "It will taste much better now, West."

Despairingly I asked, "Anything else in that bag of tricks?"

Jan rummaged around, "There is a shirt and a book," he continued his task without looking up, "and a razor."

"Pity it's a safety one or I could have cut my throat and saved myself the pain of not having to eat that...." I pointed at the tablet.

The darkness came suddenly, no gloaming (sunset) here as at home, no smell of flowers or scent of summer, only a bland hostile landscape, and a feeling of being ever further from home.

And still the rain poured down, as did the drop in temperature. I drew my backpack to me and pulled out my shirt, "Here," I handed it to the shivering boy, clad only in black trousers and sleeveless jacket. "You must be frozen." I draped my jacket around both our shoulders, and he nodded his thanks and pulled down the same colourful bandana, that I had first seen him wear when herding the sheep in the meadow.

It was a long night. I stared out at the black leaden sky thinking the rain would never cease.

"You have rain such as this in your country," Jan asked in little more than a whisper.

"Only in the summer," I joked. "That's why it's so green and fresh."

"We have beautiful places here too."

"So I believe but I've never been able to see any, folk just won't give me the time to look."

"You mean the army?"

"And the police."

"Ah the police," Jan sighed. Silence, then from the boy, "Tell me what your country is like."

I shrugged never having thought much about it, as most people do when living there. Never having taken time to see or find out what is on their doorstep. "It has castles and lochs and...."

"Lochs? What is lochs?"

"Lochs is," I laughed, "Lochs are what you'd call lakes, you know big puddles like what we'll get in here if this bloody rain doesn't stop."

"I see."

"I wish I did, any loch will do." I sighed and closed my eyes, hoping to dream that I was home again.

At last it was morning, and the rain had stopped. Jan still slept, his head on my shoulder. I gave him a nudge. "Come on Van Winkle, time to rise and shine." He moaned, wiped his eyes with the back of his hand, shuddered and struggled to his feet.

"Morning Mister West. See the rain has stopped, we can walk again."

"Oh goody goody. How about breakfast? Anything in the sack?"

"Soup?" Jan held up a can.

"Cold soup, probably taste as good as that sh…" I stopped myself, it was not the boy's fault.

"Maybe the sun will heat it as we walk along, or better still we can heat it on my feet come midday."

Jan made a face not capable of understanding this daft Scot, and I couldn't blame him.

I shrugged out of my damp shirt. Jan handed back the shirt I had loaned him.

"We will soon be dry when the sun is hotter," he assured me grinning, while ringing out his wet bandana.

"Not as hot as my feet," I countered, lifting my backpack.

Jan took a step forward, "I will carry this, old men should save their energy for walking."

"Old man!" I exploded.

"Sorry, West." To hide his embarrassment, he shouldered the pack.

"Okay, kid I wasn't too hurt." I shoved my jacket in between his bare shoulders and the pack's straps. "Here, let an old man help you. You don't want to chaff those shoulder blades do you?"

Jan turned his head to look at me. "You are very good to me, West, I will do the same for you one day."

I laughed at his humour. "Some day? We will have to get out of this, first." I swept my hand at the surrounding hills.

"Do not worry, we do not have to climb those, but should you wish to reach Poland you will have to climb hills much higher, then your feet will be really hot," adding with a chuckle as he stepped away, "and colder."

As I followed, I had the distinct feeling things were not destined to get any better than this.

We had filled up the soldiers water bottles, and what was left of their food, now there was nothing left only the horrid muck they called tablet, of which Jan appeared to relish.

When we stopped to rest, I asked, sitting down on the still wet brown grass, "Where are we headed, Jan, is it to the village where your grandfather Petrovic lives?"

Jan dropped the backpack and sat down. "No, grandfather does not live there, he lives by himself on the hillside above the village. No one must see us, especially the soldiers."

"The soldiers!" I exclaimed glaring at him. "What soldiers? You didn't say anything about soldiers!"

"There might not be, but now and again some soldiers are, how do you say....?

"Billeted," I explained.

"Billeted. So we must not be seen, it would not be good."

"You can say that again."

"It would not..."Jan started.

"Okay," I chuckled, "I get the message."

It was close on evening when we first sighted the village, Jan pulled me roughly down, beside him pointing up the hillside to our right where a boy of similar age herded sheep towards the village. "That is Vlado he must not see us, he will tell his father."

Jan sat down from where he'd squatted to watch the boy. "We are friends. I do not wish him trouble you understand. We must not be seen."

I sat down beside him. "I understand" I would dearly have told Jan to leave me here and let me make my own way to the border, but it was impossible without his help.

It was several minutes before the shepherd boy and his flock were out of sight. Thankfully there was no dog, who may well have found us.

Jan rose. "Come, we are safe now."

I had no idea of the time, only that it would soon be dark.

Jan pointed to a log cabin on the hillside, "Grandfather Petrovic, will be pleased to see me, I am his favourite."

"I hope I am too."

Eventually we were there. Without knocking, Jan threw open the door, greeting his grandfather in his own language.

"Jan?" At this sudden interruption, the old white bearded man looked up from where he had sat reading by the fire.

Jan ran forward and wrapped his arms around his kinsman. Both I suspected telling how good it was to see one another. Eventually Jan unwrapped himself and standing back introduced me, no doubt adding a bit about my troubles etc, mainly 'etc' I supposed.

It did not take the old man long to have us both by the fire while he set out a meal. This time the soup was hot and I supped greedily.

"My grandson tells me he is helping you reach Poland?" The old man sat back in his chair by the fire puffing at an old clay pipe."

He surprised me by speaking in English. "Yes if you will permit it, sir."

The old man nodded. "Jan is old enough to know what he does."

Jan broke off a piece of bread, "I have told him what has happened back in Nego, the news has not yet reached here. There are no soldiers, they too must be back in Nego. I also told him I think grandfather Spiridon will be safe, he knows where to hide. Before I run away he told me to come here, that I would be safe."

"Until you met me," I said apologetically.

The old man filled his pipe, "I will not ask why the police and army wish to catch you, you are a foreigner after all. All I know is what Jan has told me, and what they have done to his village, with many good people dead. So I have told him he must help you. It will help to beat those who done this bad thing in Nego. You understand?"

"Yes."

The old man turned to his grandson. "You must leave early tomorrow, before the soldiers return. You will give West my climbing boots, I think they will fit, if not you know what to do."

"Cut off my toes," I chuckled.

The man stared at me seriously. "Let us hope it does not come to that, but if Jan does what he should do, you will not long be in the snow."

I gulped, wishing I had not made that joke.

With grandfather and son fast asleep I took my tattered incomplete novel from my pack. It was the first suitable opportunity I had since leaving the stricken village.

Zofia, poor Zofia, she had said 75 which I took to be the page number as I could think of nothing else it might be. Nervously I flicked through the pages, many missing by my personal, or should that be impersonal use, hoping that page 75 was still intact. It was. I drew closer to the log fire. Flames threw eerie shadows across the ceiling, and I peered closer in the firelight, slowly and carefully scanning the page, until reaching the bottom.

Disappointed at not having found anything out of the ordinary, I started at the top again, this time carefully reading each word, none of which were underlined to offer a clue.

The book on my lap I sat back in my chair, the heat of the fire tempting sleep. I drew a hand across my eyes and stared down at the novel which I had never seemed to have finished, my only conclusion, that it held some secret such as micro dot or dots, which I unwittingly was to carry back to Poland or in this case I believed home. The task no doubt that of the unfortunate Mr Malcolm. How I hated that man for his unfortunate illness and the mess however unintentional he had got me into.

Grandfather had dished up an enormous breakfast, and while we ate assembled all that we'd require for the journey, or to me more an Arctic expedition, what with ropes, ice picks, woolly hats, gloves, jerkins and above all food, all to be carried.

Jan lifted his rucksack. "I am afraid you will have to carry your own backpack, West."

"I'll try, oh little Sherpa. Grandfather, I will have Jan bring back this jerkin you have loaned me when we reach the border."

The old man shook his head, "it is an old one. Should I see it again, make sure you are still not wearing it, Okay?"

At the old man's humour I warmly shook his hand. "I don't have anything to repay either you or the boy. But if I can I will, I won't forget what you have both done for me."

"Come West, you are not yet in Poland." Jan stepped to his grandfather and hugged him, a few words passed between them, then we were on our way.

By mid morning we had divested ourselves of our outer garments. A heat haze had already risen from the hard baked ground, leaving no evidence of the recent torrential rain.

At first I coped quite well over a not too undulating terrain, it being mostly meadowland. However my hopes were dashed when in looming in front of us was nothing other than the outline of high snow capped black mountains.

"We should reach the foot of those mountains today and start our climb tomorrow," Jan spoke decisively.

I grimaced at the thought of that and my already aching feet.

The hot midday sun saw us lying shirtless on the last of the green meadowland. Through a half closed eye I watched Jan dig out some food from his pack.

He handed me a thick cut cheese sandwich. "This is good, much better than the soldiers tablet.

I took it gratefully. "Are you sure it was tablet and not what they used to clean their boots?"

Chuckling at my humour, and no doubt the vision of me chewing something used for ablutions, Jan took a bite of bread and cheese.

I pointed my sandwich at the still distant mountains. "You don't expect me to climb those big things?"

Jan threw his head back laughing. "You are so funny Mister West. Is everyone in your country so funny?"

"Only the politicians, Jan."

The boy shook his head sadly. "It would be good if it was the same here."

I caught the sadness in his voice. "The groups that met back in Nego what had they hoped to achieve, before the fight that is?" I amended.

Jan shrugged. "They hoped to start a new, how do you say... government. Now," he shrugged again this time despondently, leaving the rest unsaid.

Our repast over, reluctantly I got to my feet lifting my shirt off the grass. "I suppose we better get going, but you haven't told me do we have to climb those?" I pointed with my shirt at the mountains.

"No, my grandfather showed me a way round most of them and through the passes, but we will still have to climb, that is why grandfather gave me the rope." He pointed to the rope on his backpack.

"Okay, I'm relying on you kid, you're my last hope." We started off again, although my feet still hurt.

We in fact reached the foothills of the mountains around early evening, Jan neither having a watch or of all things a mobile phone.

"We will stay here tonight West, it is warmer than the foothills."

I was only too happy to comply.

Using both his grandfather's jerkin I was wearing and his own, together with a groundsheet he had dug out of his rucksack Jan built some sort of a shelter in between some rocks.

I stood back admiringly. "Should be warmer than that night we spent in the rain," I assured him.

"Yes. This time it will not rain."

My young companion's prediction proved correct, the night was warm and clammy, and I slept like a log, the saying I suspected referring to my wooden head.

Jan was the first up and 'doing' while I lay stifling a yawn and thinking of those big 'dods' I was soon to climb.

Breakfast over, our shelter dismantled and packed we set off, Jan whistling merrily as he strode along, a little too quickly for my liking, yet again the faster we reached the border the better.

To my relief it was only the lower slopes of the black giants that we climbed, Jan without doubt knowing his way, then again to my joy, descending through narrow passes until I began to believe I should not have to do much climbing after all. I was wrong.

Jan pointed ahead. "We cannot go round that one West, we must climb," he informed me apologetically.

"Not to worry kid you've done really well," I assured him. "Have we time for a drink a bite to eat and a sit down?" I asked optimistically, my backside already half way to the ground.

"Yes." Jan rummaged in my backpack containing most of the food. "Here," he held out his hand to me, "it is the last of the chicken grandfather gave us."

Gratefully I took it, asking, "have we enough food to last, Jan?"

His mouth full of chicken, Jan answered, "Yes if we get to the other side of *that* today," he pointed a chicken leg at my erstwhile enemy.

I picked a piece of chicken out from between my teeth, "We don't have to climb to the summit? the top,"I explained.

"No," Jan's eyes gleamed mischievously, "but almost."

"You little sh...." I made a face.

Jan giggled. "It is easier than digging a hole through it."

Tunnelling, I grinned amused, by the boy's description, *The Great Escape, eat your heart out.*

Our meagre bite and rest over, Jan guided me towards my austere looking mountain. At first it was not too bad, there being still an amount of grass to cling to. Then it all changed as would the weather I thought staring up at the scudding grey skies.

Jan too saw them. "We must get higher, so that we reach the pass, over there," he pointed above him.

Now it was all rock, and ever more sheer to me as I struggled on. A little way ahead Jan halted to discard his haversack, and tie an end of rope through a shoulder strap.

Puffing and panting with the occasional grasp thrown in, I stopped to watch what he was doing.

"I will carry the rest of the rope with me, up there," he pointed to an outcrop of rock above him. "Then I will pull up my haversack, then your backpack. Okay?"

"Then me," I joked.

"Then you," Jan said in a way that said he meant it.

With some apprehension I watched the boy climb, never understanding where he found anything to grip or hang on to, only now and again halting to hitch the rope more comfortably on his shoulders. Then he was at the top, crawling on all fours over the giant rock.

After a minutes rest and Jan reappeared, pulling up the first of our packs.

Unsure of the teenager having the strength to help haul me up I stood there waiting. Now I would soon know I choked, bending to lift the rope that had landed at my feet.

"Don't worry, West, I will not let you fall!" the boy waved assurance at me.

"You bloody well better not, I didn't come all this way to end up for archaeologists to think they had found the first fossil from North Berwick."

I took hold of the rope leaned all my weight backwards and sort of started to walk up my rock, doing well until meeting my first obstruction in the form of a small rock overhang. How the hell had the boy got over this? It hadn't seemed anything from where I had stood below?

Now I could not see Jan, only his voice telling me to swing myself out and away from the rock and he would pull me up.

For a moment I hung there, not at all convinced that a slightly built fourteen year old could take my weight far less pull me up, and although the drop, should I fall was not great, to break a leg or any other limb would seriously hamper my chances of ever reaching my destination.

However I could not hang around here all day I thought, with no pun intended. I had to make the effort, my only decision was whether to close my eyes or not when I swung away from the rock. Also my fear was that my weight and momentum might pull Jan down as well.

I took a deep breath, mimed a 'here goes' and propelled myself outward into space.

I felt a jerk on the rope and flew back towards the rock, another jerk and I was pulled free.

I had made it, or more accurately Jan had made it, for now I was on the opposite side of the rock from where I had started, and with one gulp of fresh air began, with the aid of Jan, to pull myself up to where he stood.

"You have done it, West. I knew you could!" Jan jubilantly shouted at me lying struggling for breath, and a little relief.

Shaking I rose to my feet. "*You* did it Jan, not me, if I ever get across the border it will be because of you!"

Embarrassed Jan wound up the rope. "There is still some distance to travel, but I think now we will succeed. That is the right word?"

"You bet, Jan you bet it's the right word," and I slapped him on the back in emphasis.

Chapter 12

The grey clouds that I witnessed earlier thankfully came to nothing, although up here on our side of the mountain a chill wind blew. Up ahead picking the best route for me to follow as usual, Jan drew to a halt. "Can you climb a little more, West?"

I drew up following his pointing finger at the massive before us. "Chr....!" I stopped myself in time, "it's that high, I'd be afraid to say God in case I got an answer. It's even higher than the cost of living!" To say I was appalled by this insurmountable obstacle would be an understatement.

Jan was amused by my distress, and despite what he had done for me I could have thumped him one.

Anticipating my intention and still grinning Jan took a hasty step back. "It is all Okay West, we will climb round it."

"You wee bugger, you did that on purpose." Now I too was grinning, but my grin was not out of humour but downright sheer relief.

As Jan had said we made our way round the black ominous mountain instead of attempting to climb over it. It was as we reached a shoulder of this great lump, that Jan as usual in front drew to a halt, shouting and calling out excitedly to me. Quickening my pace I caught up with him.

"Look! Down there, West! Down there!"

Catching his excitement I too looked to where he pointed.

"It is Poland, West! That is Poland!"

I choked back my relief. Poland at last was within my reach. "You've done it Jan, you've done it." I slapped him on the back.

Perhaps it was the excitement that I had visions of my meeting Fenton again, him scolding me for being so stupid at having got myself into such a situation, that I failed to properly grasp the rock in order to pull myself up and over it when we started the last leg of our journey, and before I knew it I was falling, sliding and bumping down the side of the rock vaguely aware of Jan's terrified voice somewhere in the background above me.

Finally I reached the foot, and lay there cursing my own stupidity. I rolled onto my back to inspect the damage. I was now in fashion with teenagers, white knees showing through the tears in my trousers, my only trousers, the ones I had worn since leaving home. Pain leaped at me from somewhere in the area of my right ankle. Chr... all I needed was a broken ankle. I cursed again, *not now, not when within sight of my destination.*

Smalls stones rumbled past closely followed by an anxious teenager. "West! You are all right?" he kneeled down scanning me for any sign of injury.

I leaned awkwardly forward and gently grasped my injured ankle, the throbbing now having changed to downright pain.

"It is your ankle. Is it broken, West?"

"I don't know, pal. If it is I am well and truly buggered." I spat out the words in contempt of myself and my own carelessness.

Kneeling beside me Jan stared up at the rock from where I had fallen, distress etched on his young face. "How am I to get you back over there, West, if you cannot walk?"

Anger now replaced my pain. "We didn't come all this way to be stopped now, pal. Help me up and I will give it a try. The rock now looking as did my ankle twice its normal size.

It did not take long to find out realization fell short of determination, there was no way I was ever going to reach the top of this confounded 'dod' of rock. Less than a quarter way up, and despite all of Jan's efforts, I had to admit defeat.

Jan sat where I had ground to a halt in what would be described as a ledge, his look one of concern as well I should think of disappointment for me.

"We must rest." Jan bent forward and pulled up my trouser leg to reveal an ankle twice its normal size. "You cannot climb further, at least not today. I will make a shelter here for us both and perhaps tomorrow we can start again."

Despondently I shook my head, all too aware of the boy's reasoning. "Yes, maybe I can give it another go tomorrow, if the swelling goes down." I turned my face up to the sun. "And there's still enough daylight to have travelled that wee bit further today, even to Poland where you would have gotten rid of me."

I couldn't tell whether the boy understood me or not, but suddenly his face changed and he looked away. "Where I must leave you and return to find both my grandfathers."

At the sadness in the boy's voice I felt ashamed. This kid had more to worry about than my swollen ankle. And the quicker he got me to the border and got himself back to both villages the better.

Shakily and holding on to the rock I got up. "Come on kid let's try a wee bit more, for I'm buggered if I'm going to let this big lump come between us and down there," I pointed to the border.

It was almost dark by the time I saw the top of my own 'Everest', Jan marvelling at my determination, though to be fair it was more to do with desperation to be down out of the encroaching wind and cold.

At last, leaning and propped up by Jan who constantly had to return for our packs we reached the bottom, this time on the opposite and correct side.

I sat my back against a rock outcrop watching the boy's endless energy as he laboured to build our shelter for the night.

Away on the distant horizon I caught a brief flash of light, Jan explaining it came from cars on a highway on the Polish side. My heart skipped a beat, I was almost there.

It did not rain during the night and here on the flat land at the foot of the mountain sheltered from the wind it was really quite hot in the morning sun.

"How much food is left, Jan?"

"Enough," he replied shoving a few things back into our packs.

I stopped what he was doing, "I mean is there enough food as you say for you? For your return. You do intend going back?"

Jan nodded. "I must know what has happened to my grandparents, you will understand."

"You will have enough food?" I insisted upon asking.

"Yes grandfather understood this."

I refrained from insulting the boy by asking how he would manage on his own, not when I witnessed how he had climbed the steepest parts by himself on the way here.

Finished packing Jan stood up, facing me. "Perhaps you should take your boot off to ease the pain?"

He knelt down and I shouted, louder than intended, "No Jan my ankle will swell even more and I won't get my boot back on! Leave it!"

Startled by my rebuke Jan took a hasty step back, and I instantly regretted my reaction.

"Sorry kid, I didn't mean to shout. I'm just an old bad tempered wrinkly."

My expression puzzled the boy who was now wary of me, and that my injury may have affected what little brain I had.

"I will go down there amongst the trees and bring back a stick for you to lean on." he quietly informed me clearly still smarting from my unexpected rebuke.

Jan turned. "Sorry kid," I apologised, "what I said was uncalled for."

He turned round. "Okay, I'll get you a stick, and if you shout at me again I will kick it away when you are leaning on it." His laughter followed him as he left.

I sat there my back propped against a rock staring up at a cloudless sky, then to the border less than a mile away. Soon I'd be home, with all the things I had taken for granted. A walk along the beach at North Berwick, the sound of children's laughter the smell of the sea, ice cream, I licked my lips in anticipation, my brother telling me off about how daft I was. Little things like that, I laughed. How lucky I was and many of my fellow countrymen in comparison to that of the kid who had helped me here. What was his life to be? Back to a burned out village with many of his neighbours dead or injured, similarly both his grandparents. So what the hell was *I* moaning about?

"West!" I had not heard my wee guide returning. I must have dozed off.

He stood there holding out a trimmed branch to me. "It is big enough, Yes?"

I took it from him and leaned on it as it were a walking stick and not a crutch. "Yes, Jan it will do."

Jan stood, a puzzled look on his face, for he too had heard the sound of approaching feet on gravel. I looked to where the sound had emanated, and a boy of around Jan's age appeared, closely followed by a figure I did know and that was of Serge.

"Serge!" I explained, "You escaped from the village?" my first reaction as why he was here at all, and at having found us.

Serge pushed his young companion in our direction, Jan calling out the boy's name, whose face I now saw to be covered in bruises.

Jan spoke to me while still looking at the boy," It is my friend Vlado."

I took a step forward with the intention of greeting Serge until I saw the gun pointed at me.

"Stay where you are West if you know what's good for you."

Unable to understand the situation and especially Serge, I asked "What's all this about Serge? Why the gun? And why are you here?" I pointed at the boy,"And what has happened to that laddie's face?"

"He hit me mister, made me bring him here," Vlado sounded scared, dead scared. "Jan, he beat up your granddad, who would not tell him where you and your friend was."

"His name's Barns, moron," Serge chastised the boy, "It's true the old man wouldn't tell, then your little pal happened to call and when I threatened to beat him up, the old man decided to talk." Serge laughed sarcastically.

"So what's the story Serge?" I flicked a hand. "And why follow me here?"

Serge beamed at me, "You still don't get it Barns, do you?"

"Then tell me, Serge, what don't I get?"

"Who do you think organised the raid on the village?" His face lit with self admiration.

"So it's you that's the traitor, you never meant me to get out the country, did you Serge?

But you knew the whereabouts of all the Groups, Mark's….."

"Not all of them." Serge appeared amused at being in full control of the situation. "It was much easier to wait until all the Groups met."

"And have them massacred," I butted in.

Serge shrugged, "Something like that."

"So it wasn't Andrias who tried to shoot me back in the village, it was you that was behind me that shot him."

"Got it in one, West Barns."

"And Zofia? Was she killed by the soldiers?" I halted at Serge's shake of his head. "But you were her boyfriend! She trusted you for god sake!"

"Zofia was a fool. However, she did tell me that last morning about your book. She was afraid you might take the offer by a man in the village to take you to Poland, and should he fail, you and the book could fall into the wrong hands."

"But how did you know where I went after I escaped from the village?"

"I was fortunate to see you and this little man here," he waved his gun at Jan, "Climb over the wall. Later I came across his grandfather who I recognised as the one that we and this one here had a drink with one night. He trusted me."

I nodded remembering seeing them the night I had spoken with Zofia and the little man who had offered to take me to Poland.

Serge continued, "Your grandfather very obligingly told me where he believed you to be headed, he was right. I took the road which you two could not take without first driving through the village which you couldn't do without having your arses shot off, so you had to take the long mountain road. Hence my reason for reaching Clu just a little behind your departure. The rest you know." Serge lifted his arm in triumph, "so here I am."

At the mention of his grandfathers' and what this evil man had most likely done to both of them, I had to grab Jan by the shoulder before he launched himself at the man.

Sobbing, Jan walked slowly to where his friend stood, and I was afraid it was only a ploy to get closer to his enemy.

Jan's eyes met mine and I read there what he meant to do. I closed my eyes and slowly shook my head hoping he would understand that I meant him not to do anything, for this man had already betrayed and killed, and another two or three would make little difference to him.

Suddenly Serge appeared to grow tired of it all. "Now mister foreign gentleman, let's say I am here for a reason, and that reason is the book which you carry."

Now some of it seemed to fit, but not all. "Why should my book interest you? It's not the type of book that you'd read, the goodies win in the end."

"Very witty my friend," Serge smirked. "Now, the book if you please. I cannot have you telling the world lies about my country and what is happening here."

"And if I don't please?"

"Then I will shoot you and your little friends and take the book anyway."

Both boys stood terrified and I was not so very far behind. The last thing I wanted was to see the youngsters hurt.

I stooped to lift my backpack. "Okay. But first let the boys go."

Serge shook his head, "There is information in the book Mr Malcom would have taken back...lies about my country and what is happening here. I cannot allow that to happen. I make the rules, Barns."

"So what happens after you have the book, kill us all?"

What I said had only made things worse for the boys. I loosened the straps of my pack and first threw my spare shirt on the grass, Serge waving his gun impatiently, in an effort to make me hurry.

"Ah here it is!" I drew the book from the backpack. "All this trouble for…" I threw the book at him and while his eyes were on its flight, I fired my borrowed police pistol, taking the traitor in the chest.

Serge had only a few seconds to stare at me with incomprehensible eyes, before he dropped to the ground.

I heard a squeak. The sound came from Vlado, his eyes riveted on the dead man, as if waiting for him to rise.

Jan stepped beside him, and looking at the body declared with a nod, "You did well mister West. You saved our lives."

"And you mine, Jan."

Epilogue

"Are you sure you will not come with me to Poland?"

Jan shook his head. "This is my country, I must stay to make things better."

Leaning on my makeshift walking stick I hobbled by his side. "Your grandfathers, can I send you and them some money?"

"Not for a while. I think I will live in Clu with my grandfather Petrovic. It will be safer."

"Then I will send it there."

"No, West, I am pleased to have helped you, now you can help all of us by taking home your book, whatever is important in it. Besides, it is safer for me that no one knows that I have helped you. Yes?"

Disappointed that I could not help the boy, and who no doubt was in need of it, I agreed. I held out my hand, "Hope to see you again Jan Petrovic, only this time you come to *my* country," I smiled.

Instead of returning the handshake, Jan threw his arms around my neck. "Goodbye mister West Barns. Someday I will see you again." he threw out his chest, "when I am president of my country."

Still laughing, Jan turned to meet his waiting friend, and I had no fears on their making it safely back home, and that someday Jan would indeed be his country's president.

A little later I hobbled past the white stones marking the border. I had reached Poland. My nightmare was at an end I was no longer *persona non grata*.

Printed in Poland
by Amazon Fulfillment
Poland Sp. z o.o., Wrocław

64034259R00078